# A Special Signed
# Hardback Edition of

# THE LAST PANTHEON

## limited to just 60 numbered copies

Tade Thompson

Nick Wood

This is number: 31

# THE LAST PANTHEON

*To John Jodle,*

*Jobe [signature]*

# THE LAST PANTHEON

## Tade Thompson and Nick Wood

### *With illustrations by Tade Thompson*

NewCon Press
England

Published in April 2024 by NewCon Press,
41 Wheatsheaf Road, Alconbury Weston, Cambs, PE28 4LF

NCP322 (limited edition hardback)
NCP323 (softback)

10 9 8 7 6 5 4 3 2 1

ISBN:
978-1-914953-71-2 (hardback)
978-1-914953-72-9 (softback)

Cover image by Tade Thompson
Cover design by Ian Whates
Internal illustrations by Tade Thompson

Editorial meddling by Ian Whates
Typesetting by Ian Whates

# INTRODUCTION

## Tade Thompson

What you're holding in your hand is an artifact.

Back in 2013, Nick Wood and I started a long-running discussion about 1970s superheroes in Africa, and that conversation culminated in this novella.

I'm writing this ten years later, in 2023, and Nick is, sadly, no longer with us. The current format is what we imagined: a short and sharp illustrated book that wears Silver Age comics bonafides on its sleeve.

It represents our early work and, as you can imagine, having grown as a writer, I had an intense urge to rewrite a lot of it. But discussions with writer friends led to my decision to leave it as is, a crystallisation of our skill and ruminations at the time of writing. Besides, I wouldn't want to rewrite Nick's prose, and it would be unfair if I only polished my stuff. So here it is, warts and all.

The art is new.

If you have any problems with the illustrations, blame me, but also, indulge me. I am not a professional artist, just a motivated amateur.

There's more context in the backmatter for those interested, otherwise, flip the page. I hope you enjoy this glimpse of superhero weirdness.

*—Tade Thompson, London*
*November 2023*

# IN MEMORIAM

## Tade Thomson
### [Originally written for SFWA]

Nick and I met about 12 years ago. We were in an anthology together and there was a mutual "I see what you did there" moment when we commented on each other's stories.

We quickly discovered a love of old African superhero comics, specifically Mighty Man (South Africa) and Powerman (Nigeria - renamed Powerbolt for Western audiences). We had long, twisty conversations about superheroes, African literature, politics, how the Cold War played out in different parts of Africa, uranium, Patrice Lumumba, philosophy, and a host of other topics, all over email or Skype. He was extremely well-read and yet still curious when we swapped book recommendations. We met each other's families. We collaborated on both fiction and non-fiction.

We both worked in what you might call the Mind Sciences, him a clinical psychologist, me a Consultant psychiatrist, and he often sent me scientific articles like an older colleague should.

I consider him part of the first wave of modern African science fiction, and his seminal novel *Azanian Bridges* encapsulates a lot of his egalitarian ideas. Ursula le Guin called it 'chilling and fascinating, and a pleasure to read'.

In our talks I discovered he'd had a whole other life as a journalist and an advocate for equality in 1980s South Africa. He'd taught underprivileged people. He once wrote fiction where he donated all of the proceeds to charity. He'd worked with children at risk of suicide. He was a person who cared by doing, not talking.

There's a saying that you can achieve anything if you're willing to let others have the credit. My experience with Nick is that he was always willing to do that. He would let his name be second on published papers because he seemed to genuinely enjoy the success of others. Nick was the first person to send me a review of my novels when they came out. I still have screenshots of my own work from him. He got to them before my agent or mother did.

The thing about Nick is he smiled all the time, which, when you consider the perspective of his chronic pain, was pretty amazing. He'd ask me to 'pop in for coffee and cake' any time I was anywhere near his post code. He knew I wrote longhand and he would always suggest these handwriting-to-text apps or websites.

*Water Must Fall*, his 2020 novel, was Nick all over. He went all in on a topic that was close to his heart: climate change. He was Solarpunk before it became a thing.

The last piece of writing he sent me was in 2022, a paper on the psychological consequences of climate change. He told me he'd stopped writing fiction. He said, "My fiction wasn't going anywhere, so I've given up." Which is the saddest sentence I ever heard from him. But even then, at that low ebb, he was still encouraging me.

He was brilliant, gentle, and a science fiction writer through-and-through.

Remember Nick Wood.

# A Special Signed
# Hardback Edition of

# THE LAST PANTHEON

## limited to just 60 numbered copies

Tade Thompson

Nick Wood

This is number: 31

# THE LAST PANTHEON

To John Jroule,

Joe

# THE LAST PANTHEON

## Tade Thompson and Nick Wood

*With illustrations by Tade Thompson*

NewCon Press
England

Published in April 2024 by NewCon Press,
41 Wheatsheaf Road, Alconbury Weston, Cambs, PE28 4LF

NCP322 (limited edition hardback)
NCP323 (softback)

10 9 8 7 6 5 4 3 2 1

ISBN:
978-1-914953-71-2 (hardback)
978-1-914953-72-9 (softback)

Cover image by Tade Thompson
Cover design by Ian Whates
Internal illustrations by Tade Thompson

Editorial meddling by Ian Whates
Typesetting by Ian Whates

# INTRODUCTION

## Tade Thompson

What you're holding in your hand is an artifact.

Back in 2013, Nick Wood and I started a long-running discussion about 1970s superheroes in Africa, and that conversation culminated in this novella.

I'm writing this ten years later, in 2023, and Nick is, sadly, no longer with us. The current format is what we imagined: a short and sharp illustrated book that wears Silver Age comics bonafides on its sleeve.

It represents our early work and, as you can imagine, having grown as a writer, I had an intense urge to rewrite a lot of it. But discussions with writer friends led to my decision to leave it as is, a crystallisation of our skill and ruminations at the time of writing. Besides, I wouldn't want to rewrite Nick's prose, and it would be unfair if I only polished my stuff. So here it is, warts and all.

The art is new.

If you have any problems with the illustrations, blame me, but also, indulge me. I am not a professional artist, just a motivated amateur.

There's more context in the backmatter for those interested, otherwise, flip the page. I hope you enjoy this glimpse of superhero weirdness.

*—Tade Thompson, London*
*November 2023*

# IN MEMORIAM

## Tade Thomson
[Originally written for SFWA]

Nick and I met about 12 years ago. We were in an anthology together and there was a mutual "I see what you did there" moment when we commented on each other's stories.

We quickly discovered a love of old African superhero comics, specifically Mighty Man (South Africa) and Powerman (Nigeria - renamed Powerbolt for Western audiences). We had long, twisty conversations about superheroes, African literature, politics, how the Cold War played out in different parts of Africa, uranium, Patrice Lumumba, philosophy, and a host of other topics, all over email or Skype. He was extremely well-read and yet still curious when we swapped book recommendations. We met each other's families. We collaborated on both fiction and non-fiction.

We both worked in what you might call the Mind Sciences, him a clinical psychologist, me a Consultant psychiatrist, and he often sent me scientific articles like an older colleague should.

I consider him part of the first wave of modern African science fiction, and his seminal novel *Azanian Bridges* encapsulates a lot of his egalitarian ideas. Ursula le Guin called it 'chilling and fascinating, and a pleasure to read'.

In our talks I discovered he'd had a whole other life as a journalist and an advocate for equality in 1980s South Africa. He'd taught underprivileged people. He once wrote fiction where he donated all of the proceeds to charity. He'd worked with children at risk of suicide. He was a person who cared by doing, not talking.

There's a saying that you can achieve anything if you're willing to let others have the credit. My experience with Nick is that he was always willing to do that. He would let his name be second on published papers because he seemed to genuinely enjoy the success of others. Nick was the first person to send me a review of my novels when they came out. I still have screenshots of my own work from him. He got to them before my agent or mother did.

The thing about Nick is he smiled all the time, which, when you consider the perspective of his chronic pain, was pretty amazing. He'd ask me to 'pop in for coffee and cake' any time I was anywhere near his post code. He knew I wrote longhand and he would always suggest these handwriting-to-text apps or websites.

*Water Must Fall*, his 2020 novel, was Nick all over. He went all in on a topic that was close to his heart: climate change. He was Solarpunk before it became a thing.

The last piece of writing he sent me was in 2022, a paper on the psychological consequences of climate change. He told me he'd stopped writing fiction. He said, "My fiction wasn't going anywhere, so I've given up." Which is the saddest sentence I ever heard from him. But even then, at that low ebb, he was still encouraging me.

He was brilliant, gentle, and a science fiction writer through-and-through.

Remember Nick Wood.

# PROLOGUE

**February 18, 1979**
Sahara Desert, Africa

*My hands are deep in sand, and there is blood on the snow.*

He did not know why there was snow.

He tried to rise, but it was not time. His breath came in ragged gasps, a death rattle? His ribs grated on each other when he inspired. His jaw felt heavy and swollen. More drops of blood on the snow, from his face. He tried to move his tongue, but it had grown snug inside his mouth and did not budge.

He was on all fours. He could tell that now, but his right arm was crooked, maybe broken and bent out of shape. The left arm held all the weight. Another warm dribble down his face. He pulled the left arm out of the snow and wiped it across his face. It came back smeared red.

He tried again to stand, but it hurt, a pervasive pain that he had never experienced, his nerves screaming for respite. It seemed like he could feel the individual links on his backbone.

*What happened? What did I do? What did we do? Why is it snowing?*

He managed to stand. The horizon wobbled and turned, or he may have been turning. It was difficult to tell. Blood still streamed out of him, dripping on his chest and landing on the snow. He felt neither heat nor cold, but the crisp air helped to clear his head and stabilise his vision.

There were depressions in the snow, footsteps, ending in a lump of a man about fifty yards away. Head bowed, arms by the side, kneeling. His enemy.

Snowflakes gently dropping to earth.

*Oh, mother. What have we done this time?*

He could not find any hatred inside himself, not anymore. He was done. This was over.

He tried to fly away, but his feet stayed linked to the earth. He could not jump because each movement was agony, especially for his right arm.

Maybe he was dying.

He focused on the weather. It should not be snowing. He closed his eyes and coaxed the clouds and asked the water to disperse. You didn't force weather; you just eased it into doing what it wanted. You said, please don't form precipitation. Sometimes, it listened.

The snowfall stopped but the clouds would not move. Not yet.

Breathing heavily now. The next part would hurt, but had to be done. He held his right forearm and twisted counter-clockwise sharply. He screamed, almost passed out again.

His enemy did not stir.

Bastard.

Maybe there was some hatred left after all.

He took strips of his enemy's cape and made a crude sling, then he walked away.

After an hour he came to a gaggle of Algerian troops. By then the sun had returned and the snow had turned to slush. They recognised him and eased safeties off their weapons. He took their fear, absorbed it and fed it to his body for healing.

He spoke Arabic by drawing it out of their minds.

'I surrender,' he said. 'Take me to prison.'

# ONE

## 2014

Kokoro had aged well, he thought, but then he missed the question she asked.

"I'm sorry, could you repeat that?"

"I said the blogsphere wonders why you chose crime with your abilities, rather than more noble actions like those of Black Power."

"Ah... I see. Well, I don't think anyone wakes up and decides to be a criminal, Miss Kokoro. A number of things happen, inconsequential nudges, impressions, and time passes. One day you wake up to find out that you are not the hero of your own story. When the newspapers describe you as "the international criminal known only as the Pan-African" you realise you've been cast and typecast even. There is a power in naming things. You become the name and you convince yourself that it fits like an old coat."

Behind the lights technicians in the studio moved, dark shadows keeping the television machine going. He saw his own image on one of the monitors. He sat opposite Elizabeth Kokoro and to his left the network had erected a massive black-and-white poster of him taken from 1975 in his Pan-African war paint. He sported an Afro back then and his expression was feral, possessed. He had a fury that time and prison leached out of him.

No, it wasn't prison that took the rage away. It was that last time in the Sahara.

"Thunderclap344 from Zimbabwe asks why you didn't break out of prison," said Kokoro. He wondered why she had no tablet or clipboard. She had told him this segment of the interview

11

would be a live Q and A from the web. Where was she reading the questions from? Probably the producer was feeding her by a plug in her ear.

"I had no reason to. From the moment I retired I was determined to rejoin society. That meant taking responsibility for what I had done. I surrendered to the Algerian authorities, but it turned out that I had never really committed any crimes in Algeria besides illegally crossing their borders and violating their airspace. They were quite nice to me, considering. Extradition was a nightmare. South Africa tried to claim me, but the whole Apartheid thing meant nobody listened to their noise. Nigeria began extradition proceedings but gave up in 1983 because there was a coup. Ghana, Morocco, Gambia… so many prisons, so little time."

Kokoro adjusted her skirt. She knew all this, but managed to maintain an expression of curious interest. Good interviewers had that quality of not representing themselves, but the listener.

"I ended up in your fine country. Incarcerated for thirty years in Edo City."

"When did you leave jail?"

"I've been free since 2003."

"What have you been doing since then?"

What indeed.

## 2003

The clerk was old, way past retirement, and officious. He had one of those Mugabe moustaches that reminded you of Hitler. If he knew who the Pan-African was he did not indicate. He passed forms through the gap in the window with large blue 'x's marked at the points requiring signature or thumb print.

"What's this?" asked the Pan-African.

"This confirms that your personal effects were returned to you in the same condition as the day you entered, with the exclusion of any perishable goods and age-related changes."

"I didn't enter with any personal effects."

"So nothing was returned to you. Is the nothing in the same condition?"

The Pan-African stared.

"That was a joke," the clerk said, in a flat voice.

"I see."

"You still have to sign."

He signed.

The clerk gave him sixty-five American dollars.

"What's this?"

"Something the government gives to rehabilitated offenders to help them start off in their new life. Congratulations. Your debt to society is paid. Go forth and live a virtuous life."

The clerk stamped a final form and handed it to him.

Outside. The gates slammed shut with an electrical whine.

Nobody waiting. No friends, no family.

Edo City Prison was technically outside city limits, but nobody cared as long as the degenerates were out of sight. All around him was bush, bisected by a single black-top road which led to civilisation.

*I am Tope Adedoyin. I used to be called the Pan-African. I was in prison, but now I am free. I have a piece of paper that says I am free. It has an official stamp on it. I'm free.*

He looked at his feet. Black Hush Puppies from aeons ago, fashionable if he were someone's grandfather. He tested something, focused, and left the ground behind. Two, three feet in the air, hovering, testing. Then he fell back down. It was like swimming; you had to relearn how to hold your breath.

He started walking north along the side of the road. Cars and lorries swept past, dusting him. He considered trying to hitch a ride, but thought better of it. He wanted to be alone and charity brought with it the necessity to reciprocate with conversation.

He stopped to relieve his bladder and noticed a footpath, part obscured by weed growth, but definitely a walkway. He zipped up and followed it, not knowing why. A whim, a notion of delight or despair. The sound of traffic faded. He passed a yellowed wooden sign, a placard rendered blank by acid rain. He soon came to a settlement. It was a rag-tag collection of shacks, shanties and lean-tos.

It was probably illegal. The shanty town could not be seen from the road, which meant no taxes or police. There were no estates close by, no legitimate citizens for them to contaminate, and there was no impending property development. These were the criminals, the drunks, the dangerous psychotics; the detritus of society, both victims and perpetuators. The poor were the greatest sinners in a free enterprise society.

Would it be a violation of his parole if he lived here?

He encountered the insensate form of a drunk, which he stepped over. The first dwelling was a beer parlour with 'No Cridit' stencilled in red paint. A lone male customer drank *kai kai*, local gin, which was more wood alcohol than ethanol.

"Good evening, uncle," said Tope. "May I join you?"

"Good evening, my son," said the old man. He pulled a seat out by way of invitation. "Sadia! Bring another glass."

Tope sat down, accepted one glass and drank in silence. He called to Sadia and asked for a Stout and another half-litre of gin for the old man. If they noticed his distorted arm they did not draw attention to it.

"I'm looking for a place to stay," said Tope.

"That's what I said when I arrived here," said the old man. "I was twenty and I had just killed a man. Have you killed anyone?"

Tope had a flashback. He... he...

*He bunched the ridiculous cape in his left hand and pulled Black-Power towards himself and punched his head into the desert sand. Black-Power's arms twitched in an epileptic fit. The Pan-African stamped on that head. The sand became red with blood.*

"No," said Tope. "I haven't killed anyone."

Over the next few days he built a house out of wood from trees he chopped down himself and nails he scavenged and corrugated iron he found. He didn't mind. It kept him busy and was not taxing at all. At first they did not know who he was, but a

14

boy saw him levitating in order to reach a difficult part of his roof.

Once they knew the Pan-African was among them, his power grew and he fixed their weak and wobbly dwellings. He helped till the land on their untaxed farms. The sheer number of the diseased among them complicated matters and added a dark shade to his power. The hepatitis and AIDS dementia, the heart failures and septic abortions. The power from the sufferers was tainted, sick power that could turn him to mischief again if he let it.

"I just kept busy with this and that," said Tope.

Elizabeth nodded. "Another question from the forums: what did you learn from your days as the Pan-African?"

"Crime does not pay, stay in school, and never, ever get into a fight with a man who wears a cape because such a man is insane."

"Now you're just being flippant."

"Only half flippant. Seriously, have you looked at the costume that idiot used to wear? I almost killed him with the damn thing."

"Then why didn't you? You fought many times and both walked away to tell the tale."

"I wasn't trying to kill," said Tope. "I was trying to teach."

"To teach what?"

"That Black-Power, with all his good intentions, was part of the problem, not the solution."

"We'll come back to that, but I have another question, this from Powerfan565. She asks why you were called the Pan-African Coward in 1975."

Tope sighed. He knew this would come up.

"I don't remember."

"Powerfan565 says, was it not because the first time you bumped into Black-Power you ran away?"

"No comment."

"Did you run away from him?"

"No comment." Tope took a sip of water from the glass beside him. He maintained eye-contact with Elizabeth.

"This is supposed to be frank interview," she said.

"I can explain," said Tope, "but I'm not going to. No comment."

"We have a caller on the line. Caller you're live on Flashback. Go ahead."

The voice came through on the studio speakers and chilled Tope to his core. He could actually feel pain in his chest where he had received the hardest hit in the desert.

"Pan-African, is there something you think you're qualified to say about me?" asked Black-Power.

# TWO:
# THE POWER AWAKES

## 2014

Pain, there was always the pain.

Detective Sipho Cele grunted as he stood up from his desk, holding his arm tightly over the right side of his body. Such an action muted the sharp reminder of shattered ribs from decades ago, the pain at least dulling with the spread of his stomach and the slow creep of age.

He stepped around his broad desk with its bronze name plate, littered with photos and files of low lives, murderers, rapists and *tsotsis*. The scum of the Earth, so many of them, a never-ending wave that he had spent his life fighting against. But, like the hydra, you take one down and two more step into their place.

Making his way to the window, he smiled at his clever classical allusion; he was no wet-eared *plaasjapie*, as the *boere* used to say, no, he was urban smart – and old.

Much older than he looked, even though his hair was starting to pepper with grey.

As he stared down seven storeys onto the milling street below, he felt yet older still. Offices stretched high into the sky, glassed front, left and right, inscrutable – but the street itself below was teeming with people; trade and spill-off from the nearby tourist trap of Greenmarket Square.

Of the Mountain itself there was no sign, hidden behind tiers of stone and glass.

He watched the people move and bustle, a dance troupe setting up in the paved boulevard, Adderley street flower sellers spilling across for more business as an impromptu crowd gathered.

And, with vision an eagle would have been proud of, he noticed a thin young man spiralling around the crowd's edge, deftly picking back-pockets and coats.

Tcchhaaa, small fry!

There was a time when he would have shown no mercy, when his tolerance was ever set at zero.

Those were old times, gone times.

Sipho turned away with a growl of fury, making his way back to his desk, accidentally brushing past a lurid black, green and yellow cape hanging on the coat stand. He felt a faint frisson of excitement.

No.

Gone times.

Now, at least the pain was dull, hovering in the background, in places he could ignore.

The smaller desk in the corner of the room, with its tiny black swivel chair, was empty.

Where the hell was she? Thembeka took off too much time to go shopping; he would chide her when she got back. He could see the lights on her phone console glowing hot with waiting calls or people depositing urgent messages.

The door opened just as he reached his desk and was about to sit down. He hesitated, flexing his biceps involuntarily as she stepped into the room.

Sure, she was short and on the plain side, but old habits die hard. Still, he'd had to be careful; this new generation of women seemed increasingly less impressed with his towering physique and charm -- and could even cause trouble.

And, of course, she was a Xhosa, so not a real Zulu woman.

"Where have you been?" He growled, suddenly and irrationally bored with this dull city.

"Getting information off the street," she hovered in the door, watching him with hooded eyes.

"So." He sat, feeling the chair creak underneath his solid bulk. "What information do you have?"

"There's a new Super-Tik factory being set up just two streets down," Thembeka said. She looked down, as if hoping for praise, but afraid to look him in the eyes.

"Just do your job and answer the phone," he said, turning to his desktop, which was scrolling in news from all across Africa.

She sat for a moment in what felt like crushed silence and then, with an angry sigh, she picked up the phone and started speaking.

But Sipho wasn't listening. A staccato burst of noise had sprung up from the street below and he knew that sound.

Trouble.

Big trouble.

In a bound he was at the window again, gaze raking the street, missing nothing. The crowd was disintegrating rapidly, people screaming. No cops of course, a few security guards, but they were running too.

There, the central drama piece, six men standing with automatic weapons, two holding the thin young man as one large man pistol whipped him, snarling.

The boy had not been careful enough in choosing his victims.

Too bad – Detective Cele was about to turn his back too, when he noticed an old woman sidling up the street with her guide dog.

Dumb fucking dog, he was leading her into Trouble Central.

Without thinking, Sipho reached for the cape.

One of the armed men turned and shoved the woman, who fell, crying. The dumb dog sat down.

Sipho reached for the crumpled mask in his pocket, an old relic he'd never quite managed to let go, a talisman to touch, but not to wear.

The man was lifting his right boot; readying himself to kick the old woman.

Mask and cape on, Sipho Cele threw himself through the window and fell face first in a shower of glass.

*Shit*, he thought, *I can't fly.*

He panicked as the ground screamed in close to his head.

So it was that his powers finally kicked in again.

Time...

...slowed.

Or, he sped up; spinning his body deftly to land feet first, legs braced.

Fuck, those shoes had been Italian leather. They blew apart on impact, his toes splaying on buckling concrete.

One, two, three steps and he was there, catching a swinging boot before it landed against the old woman's head. He reversed the force, feeling the man's hip shatter as he was flung over backwards.

Sipho had been gentle. The man landed only ten metres away, but unfortunately on his head – and on bricked pavement.

He did not get up again, nor did he make a sound, lying there like a discarded heap of expensive clothes, as if waiting for a wash that would never come.

Sipho straightened and turned to the other men, who stood stunned, guns dangling at various angles of shock.

No... Black Power straightened and eyed the miscreants with a stony faced lack of both mercy and fear.

"Run," he growled.

So they did.

Well, four of them ran, one screaming.

The fifth man stood, a large man tattooed with prison-gang numbers, his one giant hand still holding onto the pickpocket's collar. The young man himself hung limply, spirit leaking with the blood from his broken nose. Then, abruptly, the tattooed man flung the youngster away like a crumpled piece of paper.

He slowly levelled his machine gun, a reworked AK-47 by the look of it.

His eyes were glowing red, with maddened power. *Not just tik, must be the new Super-Tik,* thought Black Power.

"Die, motherfucker..." the man opened fire.

22

Black Power covered his eyes with his left hand, bracing himself. Owwwwww, he kept the groans inside his head -- he was going to end up with a hell of a bruising on his body.

Abruptly, the firing stopped.

Black Power removed his hand and grinned at the man's furrowed frown, his gaping mouth.

He gently turned around and picked up the old woman, a little so-called coloured woman, folded in fear.

"You've been a bad boy," he said, "Say sorry to Mamma – It's time we all learned to respect our elders again."

The man snarled in frightened rage and rushed forward to launch a punch with his right hand.

Black Power covered the woman softly with his arms and thrust his face forward to meet the blow, feeling knuckles crumble against his right cheekbone.

The man screamed and stepped backwards, nursing his right hand under his left armpit,; his shaved head bobbing as he bounced up and down in pain.

Black Power straightened even more. "Run."

Within seconds, the man had disappeared.

Black Power put the woman down, and slipped the dog's lead into her left hand.

"You're safe now, Mamma!" he said.

The woman smiled and nodded gratefully. Black Power gave the dog a nudge with his toe – and they wandered off quietly down the street again.

Sirens started to screech in the distance. Time to go; there was no need to compromise his identity, hidden for so long.

But a quick and small crowd had already gathered around him.

"Who are you, mister?" an awed youngster asked.

Black Power noticed the young pickpocket crawling away out of the corner of his eye. He'd more than learned his lesson, by the look of him.

Someone was standing behind him, looking at his cape, which had been relatively undamaged.

23

"BP," read the man aloud, "British Petroleum probably, with those colours? All done as an advertisement maybe?"

The crowd glanced around, looking for cameras.

"Black Power!" he snarled, bending his legs, readying himself, scanning for his broken office window above.

Then, with a massive launch of his calves and thighs he was airborne, rocketing upward with explosive power.

*Shit*, he thought again, crashing through the remnants of his office window, rolling to a halt against the far wall.

Slowly, he untangled himself from his cape and stood up, glass crunching underneath his shredded socks.

Thembeka was standing on her desk, palms across her mouth, looking frightened.

"Who are you?" she whispered, "Who are you really?"

He offered her his hand.

"Power," he said, "Black Power."

He took her shaking hand, his slightly sweaty palm brushing her skin, and gently lowered her to the floor. "And I think you and I have some Super-Tik factories to visit."

She smiled softly, gaze dropping shyly.

He saw her startle.

He looked down. Sure, his skin was just about invulnerable, but his clothes obviously weren't. There'd been no time to dig his durable bodysuit out. There was very little left of his shirt and trousers.

"Oops," he said, turning around to her embarrassed giggle.

It was then that he heard... him.

He'd know that smooth, honey-tongued voice anywhere. His PC had locked onto a broadcast, somewhere further up the African continent.

He stepped across to his desk, it was an interview from the sound of it, a sweet feminine voice chiming in.

Old and very bad pains starting to leach back into his body at the sound of the man's voice. His ribs shrieked and his head – ached, so much so, it was hard to focus on the picture of the man

24

and woman, seated across from each other, in what looked like intimate conversation.

Thembeka stood unnoticed at his shoulder, watching too.

*That woman, the interviewer,* he thought, *she's, she's… Beautiful…* He struggled to focus on the words being exchanged between them.

Then he heard his name mentioned.

Without thinking, he reached across for the phone, dialling the number scrolling across the screen.

"…you're live on Flashback," he heard the interviewer's soft words, "go ahead."

"Pan-African," he breathed.

Pain, there's always pain.

This time, though, he would rise to greet it.

# THREE

## 2014

*Breathe. Breathe. In, out, in. Not difficult, you've been doing it all your life.*

Tope hated this, the nerves. Others might call it fear, but he had already proved himself against Black-Power. Besides, this was verbal conflict, not physical.

Elizabeth Kokoro snorted, a brief, feminine gesture, almost missed but certainly dismissive. She had always favoured Black-Power over the Pan-African and indeed there were rumours. Black-Power had been a pussy hound back then.

"Hello, brother," said Tope, voice calm.

"I am not your brother," said Black-Power, voice vibrating through the studio. Did he sound out of breath? Like he'd been running? "I am Zulu, you are Yoruba."

"And yet I still call you 'brother'," said Tope.

*You know why*, he thought.

## 15,000 B.P

"They are barely conscious," said the elder. "I can hear their left and right cerebral hemispheres arguing with each other. They think it's a god, or what they will come to think of as such when they have that concept."

"I don't know if it qualifies as consciousness," said the younger. "At least they have tools."

The primates had taken a ruminant and were gutting it. One male primate held its side where the ruminant had gored him with its horns. The elder knew he would be dead within a week from infection. They did not have an idea of religion or even death yet.

"This settlement is yours," said the younger. "I'm going further north."

"You do not wish to stay together?" asked the elder. He sounded surprised and perhaps alarmed.

"We'll be on the same continent. I will not leave the landmass or planet without letting you know, brother."

"Do not let them begin to worship you," said the elder. "We are not gods."

"I won't," said the younger.

But he did.

## 2003

"Uncle Tope, why is your arm twisted?" asked the boy.

"I broke it one time. It didn't heal well," said Tope. He hammered a nail while he spoke. On a whim he switched the hammer to the right and continued. "Works fine, though, right?"

"Right."

"Pass me the box of nails."

He stepped back and gauged the horizontality of the cross bar. He looked at the boy who nodded.

"Why do you help people?" asked the boy.

"Why do you ask so many questions?"

"My mother says I'm a question bank."

"Indeed you are," said Tope. "I shall call you "Bank" from now on."

"My mother has tribal marks," he said.

Tope looked across the way where Bank's mother tried to dredge the sluggish stream for something of value. She was twenty-four going on forty and had three horizontal scarification marks and three vertical on each cheek. It was unusual. Nobody had those any more.

"Do you want to hear a secret?" Tope asked.

Bank nodded. He was seven and had already realised that the world of adults was full of secrets. Secrets were the portal between being a child and growing up.

"You see the bar codes on the goods you buy? The black lines?"

"Yes."

"You know how the creation story of Yoruba people is Olodumare lowered Oduduwa down to the earth with sand and a chicken. The sand became the landmass and the chicken rooted around in it, scattering it all over the earth."

"I've heard this story in school, Uncle Tope."

"Well... it was a space ship. Oduduwa had something that looked like a barcode on his cheeks. There were already humans here. They saw the code and tried to copy it with their crude instruments. The barcode became the tribal marks."

Bank looked sceptical. "How do you know this?"

"I was in the space ship. I was crew."

Bank squinted, not at all filled with credulity, but still child enough to wonder.

"I'm kidding!" said Tope, though he was not.

He heard someone call his name. It was a verbal call, not a thought, and he looked up. A man was running towards the house he was repairing.

"Tope! There are tractors and police!"

"Calm down," said Tope. "Show me."

There were indeed tractors and police, but in addition there were armed Area Boys, who were local toughs usually employed by politicians to beat up the opposition. At the head of the procession was a guy in a black suit sweating in the sun, waving a sheet of paper and speaking through a megaphone.

The feedback was such that Tope could not make out what he was saying.

"What the fuck is he saying?" Tope asked the man.

"He says we should all pack up and leave within the hour otherwise the people behind him will forcibly eject us and destroy our dwellings."

"Hmm." Tope pondered a moment, then said, "Don't worry about it. Tell everyone to return to their homes and go about their daily business."

"We have nowhere to go," said the man.

"You do not need anywhere to go," said Tope. "This is your home."

He walked to the side of the road, under the shade of a palm tree, and he sat down, staring at the column invading the settlement. He began to breathe regularly, time each inspiration and expiration. He allowed his mind to reach out.

*All gods are telepathic. This is how prayer works.*

Sadia brought him a tall gourd of *ogogoro* without knowing why. He drank it in one long swallow, enjoying the burn, feeling the relaxation and disinhibition. Better than *Jonnie Walker* and *Southern Comfort* combined.

Now then.

The official.

Father of three, professional bureaucrat, one mistress currently pregnant, mortally afraid of his boss. A great love for his job, although he did not enjoy inflicting suffering on the less fortunate. *Use that.* The official stopped shouting into the public address system and shouted Marxist slogans, ordering the police to arrest the Area Boys.

Tope spread his mind further.

The Area Boys became confused. They could all see a swarm of flying ants in the air, and they scattered.

Tope nudged the police, and they ran after the Area Boys.

The machine operators screamed as the tippers and tractors became dinosaurs of the carnivorous variety.

The alcohol warmed Tope's belly. He called Bank to him and returned to his carpentry.

## 2014

"I am Zulu," repeated Black-Power. "I am not kin to you."

"You're a fucking idiot is what you are," said Tope. "You weren't helpful in the seventies and you're not helpful now."

"Hang on," said Elizabeth Kokoro. "Black-Power was a hero in his time. He was recognised all over the world. He addressed the United Nations. He saved millions from natural disasters, accidents and criminals such as yourself. How can you justify your statement?"

"Misdirection," said Tope.

"What are you talking about?" asked Black-Power.

"We've had this discussion already," said Tope. "You were too thick then and you're too thick now. You prance about in your cape and mask, a copy of your colonial master's masks by the way, not drawing inspiration from the African tradition of masking. You fly around in bright colours, puffing up your chest, chasing what, drug dealers, bank robbers, cannabis cultivators? A volcano goes off and Black-Power is there to save the day. Whoopie. What did you do that was of any long-standing significance? Not one thing. What did you do for social justice? Did you change the injustices that create the petty crime that you policed? No. Do you remember our discussions about Idi Amin? The Congo? Black-Power do you remember me telling you that Murtala Mohammed would probably be assassinated in 1976? What about Kapuuo in 1978?"

"What are you trying to say?" asked Black-Power. He did not sound so certain.

"I'm saying that you're not a hero. You were a tool of the status quo government systems. You kept the poor people in line and turned a blind eye to the real offenders. You allowed the CIA to operate with impunity throughout the continent."

"You could have stopped those same things." Black-Power sounded defensive now.

"I was not and am not a hero. I never claimed to be."

"I didn't know if —"

"Motherfucker, don't you dare. *You knew.* You knew because I told you."

"Do not make me come over there, Pan-African." The edge in his voice made Tope's momentum dry up and he could not think of anything to say. Elizabeth recovered.

"Black-Power, these are serious accusations. Do you have any comment? Any mitigating factors?"

"I have a question for the Pan-African."

"I don't go by that name any more."

"Nevertheless, I have a question."

"Proceed," said Elizabeth.

"How much are you being paid to appear on television?"

"I –" Tope started.

"That information is confidential, Black-Power. He signed a contract of non-disclosure." Elizabeth uncrossed and crossed her legs.

"I understand. But he is getting paid, no? Is this an instance of crime finally paying off? You criticise my record, but you spent your entire career trying to accumulate money. Without success, I should add. I was always there to beat you down."

"Except one time," said Tope.

"How's the arm?"

"How's your fucking chest?"

"Language, gentlemen. There are children listening," said Elizabeth. "I have a question for both of you. Biohazard344 wants to know which of you is more powerful."

"It depends," said Tope.

"It depends," said Black-Power.

"What does that mean?" asked Elizabeth.

"It means if we fly to the moon and fight we could crack it in two and still not know who is more powerful," said Black-Power.

"Speak for yourself. On the moon I would kill you," said Tope.

"Fool, you don't even have my permission to dream or fantasise about such a fight."

Elizabeth clapped her hands. "Wow! Exciting stuff. Black-Power and the Pan-African, at each other's throats again. Stay tuned: we'll be back after these commercials. If you can't wait log on to our website for behind-the-scenes streaming content."

The producer said something and they were all given five minutes off air. Elizabeth came straight for him.

"That stuff you said, was any of it true?" she asked. She wore Chanel, but he didn't think it suited her.

"All of it was true."

"Can you prove it?"

"No. Maybe. I think he was employed by the South African government at some point. I have some information that he draws a pension, but it's buried deep."

"You're quite the dark horse, aren't you? I feel we may never really know everything about the Pan-African or his motives." She flicked a hair strand and turned away.

Was she flirting with him?

# FOUR

## 2014

Detective Sipho Cele was breathing heavily. No, he must remember, *Black Power* was breathing heavily, even though his small fracas with the drug gang was receding into the history of the day.

His PC had moved on, circulating others news from Africa in a torrent of chaotic themes; crime, pleasure, sport, business – and money, always money, as the African economic giant awoke slowly, starting to face off the Chinese and the fading Yanks.

But *she* hadn't moved.

Gradually, he became aware of her small but focused presence. Thembeka, his assistant, breathing heavily at his side too – he turned to look at her.

"Was any of that true?"

"No," he said, "They're just lies from a master criminal of the past. Pan-African's super-powers, formidable though they are, don't even come close to the devious sharpness of his deluded brain."

She smiled, but he could see she didn't quite believe him.

The history of the day was just a flicker of moth wings to him.

But deeper history – well, Pan-African had reminded him of what he was ever avoiding.

Time – and accountability.

## 1961

Now that was a bad year.

Actually, that was an *esabeka* year, a year so bad it gave him nightmares still.

The year opened gently, with no hint of the tremors and traumas to come. But there were rumblings up North and – although he was growing comfortable in his Native Affairs job as a clerk in kwaMashu, near Durban – he finally decided that with great power, comes at least some small accountability.

There was a good man – an important man – in trouble, and he needed help.

Gatsha Mchunu – as he called himself then – did not want to lose his job, so he took leave and headed north. He moved rapidly, partly hanging on the backs of trains, other parts leaping across borders at night with great strides that took him hundreds of feet into the air.

His face was masked; his body encased in a plain black body-suit for night time camouflage.

*Power*, he thought, *I shall call myself Power.*

He looked down at his body and thought again, *Black* Power.

And so, at last, Black Power arrived in Katanga province of the newly independent Congolese Republic.

Elizabethville, generally a quiet and sleepy copper town he'd heard, was humming with activity and military convoys moving in and out. He saw some white faces, overheard some South African accents and knew there were mercenaries and probably South African military, as well as Katangese secessionist forces about.

By this time he was dressed in a poor, ill-fitting jacket and trousers, scuffed shoes and hat crammed down on his broad head. Masks would only attract unnecessary attention.

He was given wary directions to the airport by a few locals, who appeared to mistrust both his accent and his size.

The airport was cordoned off, so he waited for night in nearby bushes. Wet from a sudden furious burst of late afternoon warm rain, he changed out of his sodden suit.

Masked, suited and booted, he waited.

A few distant flashes of lightning lit up the dull runway.

The gods must be about.

It was then that he saw a plane had already landed.

There was no more time to wait.

He hurtled over the fence, bounded once on the tarmac and smashed through the back door of the plane.

It was a small plane, but he could smell blood on board.

Only one man stood facing him, looking startled and bemused. A white man, dressed in pilot overalls, who spoke in French.

"What do you want?" The man looked wan and tired, as if he had been ill recently.

"Where is he?"

The pilot shrugged, "They have taken him somewhere, I don't know…"

Black Power looked outside, his gaze scanning the horizon for movement. There was a flicker in the distance, a jeep heading off road.

Night fell fast in this area of the world.

He stepped outside, crouched and leapt – and in one furious bound, he was soaring over the perimeter fence.

A few troops below opened fire on him, bullets whistling past in the deepening gloom.

As he soared through the air, he watched.

The jeep was parked by a ramshackle house, roof crumbling in disrepair.

He was coming back to Earth.

Gunshots.

*Within* the house.

He crashed through the roof and landed, boots buckling wooden floorboards beneath him.

He could smell death.

Warm and recent death.

Patrice Lumumba lay, broken by boots and bullets, crumpled on his back and bayonetted too, just for good measure.

The other men in the room recoiled as dust and roof debris continued to cascade down.

Black Power took in the scene, with a cool and gathering rage.

The group were Belgians and Katangese, although they also had the background stench of the CIA hovering about them.

Two other men lay dead nearby. The man holding the bloodied bayonet was a Katangese government official he vaguely knew.

With one step forward, he snapped the man's neck with a flick of the fingers on his right hand.

He caught the dropped rifle and with one smooth motion slung the bayonet in and through the torso of a Belgian official, one who had looked the most senior, perhaps even in charge.

The man coughed bright and bubbling blood.

No one moved, stunned and frozen in disbelief.

Without a word, Black Power stooped and cradled the dead President Patrice Lumumba in his arms.

With a scream of fury he crashed through the roof again, hurtling skywards, wishing he could fly away, far away, from this chaotic, damaged Earth.

Instead, though, he ended up secretly giving the President's body to his widow, who was grief-faced and quiet, dry of tears, having already received his last words:

*"My beloved companion:*

*I write you these words not knowing whether you will receive them, when you will receive them, and whether I will still be alive when you read them. Throughout my struggle for the independence of my country, I have never doubted for a single instant that the sacred cause to which my comrades and I have dedicated our entire lives would triumph in the end. But what we wanted for our country - Its right to an honourable life, to perfect dignity, to independence with no restrictions - was never wanted by Belgian colonialism and its Western allies, who found direct and indirect, intentional and unintentional support among certain senior officials of the United Nations, that body in which we placed all our trust when we called on it for help.*

*They have corrupted some of our countrymen; they have bought others; they have done their part to distort the truth and defile our independence. What else can I say? That whether dead or alive, free or in prison by orders of the colonialists, it is not my person that is important...*

*...Neither brutal assaults, nor cruel mistreatment, nor torture have ever led me to beg for mercy, for I prefer to die with my head held high, unshakeable faith and the greatest confidence in the destiny of my country, rather than live in slavery and contempt for sacred principles. History will one day have its say; it will not be the history that is taught in the United Nations, Washington, Paris or Brussels, however, but the history taught in the countries that have rid themselves of colonialism and its puppets. Africa will write its own history and both north and south of the Sahara it will be a history full of glory and dignity.*

*Do not weep for me, my companion; I know that my country, now suffering so much, will be able to defend its independence and its freedom. Long live the Congo! Long live Africa!*

*- Patrice"*

Nineteen Sixty One, yes, now that was indeed a terrible year. The Sharpeville Massacre in South Africa had followed in March; the white apartheid State of South Africa withdrew from the Commonwealth and called itself a Republic at the end of May; the UN Secretary-General Dag Hammarskjold – he secretly knew – had indeed been shot down in skies that were to become Zambian in September of that year, but no, he would not let the litany of that dreadful year go on and on and on. Back to *now*.

## 2014

How he *hated* history and Pan-African's reminders to him of how little he had changed the course of political events within Africa.

What had *he* done, himself, apart from grow fat on his crime?

But Black Power knew his was an old justification, his fear that taking sides so sharply would end up making the political bloodshed even greater. He had dreaded the sense that he might end up carrying so much more directly the vast weight of a multitude of dead souls, who might have followed him into an ensuing and even greater conflagration.

So, instead he had straddled ideological fences through the following decades, concentrating on protecting the innocent from the smaller struggles of crime and the moral simplicities of natural disasters.

But, in the process, he had increasingly grown more doubtful of his own mission and sense of self.

The Saharan Battle in the late seventies had been the final straw – broken in body more than he would have liked to admit, he had disappeared into retirement.

Until now.

"Black Power?" Thembeka's touch on his arm was gentle, querying.

He realised with a start he had been slumped in his chair, brooding, lost in a year that had stripped his hopes and dreams away.

He smiled at her.

"We have a drug-factory to break up, don't we?"

She grinned back at him and his heart lifted.

He stood up, old aches reminding him of history yet again. 'Pan-African,' he swore to himself, 'Next time I will finish you once and for all!'

# FIVE

## 2014

The show was over. It fizzled out after the telephone fireworks with Black-Power, but Elizabeth seemed pleased. She kept taking phone calls and was unable to keep a smile off her face. Tope presumed her friends and co-workers were congratulating her. He sat in the same chair as technicians dismantled the set. They looked bored, as if they had done it a million times. A few people brought him items to autograph; a Wanted poster, an old newspaper article, a 1977 Black-Power comic showing him and Tope locked in combat with a caption that read 'THIS TIME... TO THE DEATH!' He smiled when he signed that.

"Nostalgia?" asked Elizabeth. She was at his elbow and he hadn't noticed her walk up.

"No, not really. Just amusement. These comics were propaganda tools."

"*Haba*! Now you're being completely paranoid. The comics were harmless fun aimed at children. At most they can be said to be evil for perpetuating bad art and repetitive, clichéd storylines with simplistic moral lessons." She took the comic, with its yellowed paper and handed it to the engineer, then looked up into Tope's eyes.

"You're a journalist, Miss Kokoro –"

"Call me Elizabeth."

"Elizabeth. You're a journalist. I expect better. Examine the facts. I did." He halted the engineer and took the comic back. He flipped open the first page and showed Elizabeth the copyright strip at the bottom. "See this? MKD Press. Do you know what that is?"

"No."

"I checked." Tope dismissed the engineer. "MKD Press had no local offices. The copies of Black-Power comic were shipped in regularly in large quantities on Thursday every week from England. MKD Press did have a London office, but no association with Fleet Street or United Kingdom press establishment. I followed the money. It led to Langley, to the CIA. MKD Press was generated out of Project MKDelta. Do you know what that is?"

"No, I've never heard of it."

"Have you heard of MKUltra?"

"Yes, mind control experiments that the CIA ran in the sixties and early seventies? Trying to create Manchurian Candidates, perfect assassins, human automata."

"Exactly. Only MKUltra was domestic, within the United States. MKDelta was the same program, but for foreign countries. They didn't even try to hide the association much because they didn't think anybody would look into their under-priced children's comics."

"What made you suspicious?"

"The details of the storylines were similar to encounters that Black-Power and I had. Watered down, simplified, but with facts that only he or I could know. Black-Power got his abilities from aliens and I got mine when I was struck by lightning as a child. Bullshit. Then I found what I suspected to be subliminal messages in the dialogue. I analysed the paper, the print, the ink, even the poses and body language of the characters. Many of the issues were impregnated with chemicals that might be classified as mind-altering. The comics were not harmless fun, Elizabeth."

"I think I need to know more," said Elizabeth. "Do you have time for a drink?"

"I do."

"Give me a few minutes. I'll meet you at reception when I've taken off this."

"You look quite attractive in that outfit."

She waved this away. "Stage craft. I'm better in my own clothes."

While he waited, Bank came up to him. The young man had developed a habit of walking with his face glued to his tablet, assuming he knew where he was going.

"Bank, put that thing away," said Tope.

"The money is in your account," said Bank. "These people keep their promises at least."

"That's reassuring."

"Shall we go home?"

"There's no hurry. Find us a hotel and you can take the rest of the night off."

"What are you going to do?"

"See the sights."

"You're lying."

"Go!"

"Yes, sir." With a mock salute Bank spun and left. He had not made eye-contact once during the conversation. The boy was in love with his computer.

"And call your mother to say you're not coming back tonight. I do not want her wrath."

They had excellent seats in a bar that projected out on to the lagoon. The floor-to-ceiling windows showed the water glittering with the reflection of the city lights. Elizabeth wore a sleeveless jumper and khakis. He appreciated the tautness of her muscles and the smoothness of her skin.

She drank a gin and tonic; he drank mineral water with a twist.

"No alcohol?" she asked.

"It's a school night," he said. "Mind if I ask you a question?"

"Go ahead."

"I'm not going to be so uncouth as to ask your age, but you were a reporter back in the seventies. You must be pushing sixty, but you look about thirty. What is your voodoo and how can I get some of it?"

She laughed like a girl. "Fiendish exercise, a personal dietician, workaholism and a very expensive team of plastic surgeons."

"Expensive, then."

"I forgot to add two ex-husbands."

"I'm sorry to hear that."

"Don't be. One was a cheat and the other was gay."

"I'd have thought they'd have been more discreet."

"There's no such thing, Tope. If it's in the airwaves, if it's digitised, if it's been typed, I can get to it. There are no secrets from me."

"Except in people's heads."

"Except in people's heads," she said. "But you can access that data."

"Sometimes."

"Have you read my mind?"

"No."

"Read it now."

Tope got an image of a parrot with an enormous human penis growing on its back. "Oh, you are so juvenile," he said.

She laughed. "I had to see if you were for real."

"You couldn't imagine pretty flowers and chocolate?"

"Boring."

"I suppose."

"Tope, why did you do the interview?" she asked, serious.

"For the money. You came to me, remember?"

## 2013

Tope was drinking at the beer parlour with Bank who was just old enough for liquor and a few men whose names he could not remember. They argued about the Olympics and Bolt's merits when compared with Carl Lewis.

This townie girl came up, followed by a cloud of catcalls and whistles. She wore shorts and burdened under a backpack, but there was steel in her eyes. On closer look she wasn't a girl, but her beauty was uncontested.

"Which one of you is Tope Adedoyin?"

"I'm Tope," said Bank.

"No, I'm Tope," said a man drunk from *oguro*.

A few others identified themselves as Tope and the woman sucked her teeth and turned away, generating a roar of laughter. Tope got up and went after her.

"Miss? Miss, don't mind them. I'm the one you're after. Can I help you?"

She stopped, stared him down, and squinted. "Do you remember me?"

"No, sorry," Tope said, dragging the syllables out in his uncertainty.

"Kokoro."

"Ahh, from… You used to do those reports on Black-Power."

"Yes, that's right."

"Why are you here?"

"I want to do a biopic on the Pan-African. It'll be –"

"Fuck off." Tope turned away and went back to his drink.

## 2014

"You are so stubborn! I've never seen a person so unwilling to be handed buckets of cash," said Elizabeth.

"I didn't need any money," said Tope. "I only decided to do it so that Bank and a few of the other kids from the settlement can go to university."

"How is it that the government hasn't bulldozed that settlement to the ground, anyway?"

"They've tried. Strange maladies come upon the men who carry out the orders. Sooner or later, squatters' rights will kick in. Some of this money is going to a good lawyer too."

"What happened to all the money you stole when you were the Pan-African?"

"I didn't actually steal a lot of money."

## 1975

When the dust settled in the vault, Tope inclined his head and the men loped inside to fill their bags.

"Ignore the Rands and concentrate on the gold," said Tope. "Be quick. We should be out of here within ten minutes."

The bank officials and security guards seemed oddly calm, and he would have suspected that they had set off an alarm, except he scanned their thoughts and no such thing had been done. There were no approaching police.

Tope was confused and tired. He had been fighting alongside Cubans and Chinese specialists against the South African Defence Force over Angola. He had spent the last year observing the Angolan independence from the Portuguese. When the whole quagmire descended into civil war it was impossible to decide what side to fight on. MPLA, FNLA, UNITA, what the fuck? Jonas Savimbi was a canny operator, taking support from Communist China and the United States as it suited him.

In the middle of all of this there were starving, diseased and displaced women and children. Tope had decided to help them, but he would need money, hence the excursion south to a Cape Town bank.

He heard gunfire and shattering glass.

He left the vault, went into the main banking hall and saw Alamu on the floor, skull caved in and trailing a long smear of blood that led to broken glass doors. His assault rifle was still in his hands, twisted in on itself like a strip of barbed wire.

"What's happening?" said Paulo.

"Your job is to load the gold," said Tope. "I'll deal with this."

Outside on the street the van they had planned for the getaway was flattened, like one of the cars in a compactor in a junk yard. There was a man standing on it. He wore a mask and black cape and a skin-tight body suit. And he was familiar.

"If you surrender now, you won't taste the might of Black-Power!" said the man.

It was all Tope could do not to laugh. "Brother, is that you?"

The masked man approached and recognised Tope. "What the hell is wrong with your hair?" he said.

"It's called an Afro. You know, like the Jackson Five."

"It looks ridiculous." He looked beyond Tope and saw the rest of the men. "Are you robbing this bank?"

"Brother, will you not greet me with a kiss? I haven't seen you in –"

"You were supposed to stay up north."

"I know. Things happened. I have been travelling around the world. I have much to tell you."

"You can tell me from jail. There can be only one penalty for breaking the law."

Black-Power stamped his foot and the shock wave cracked the floor and disabled the robbers, except Tope.

"Brother, there is no need for violence. This money is going to feed women and children in Angola."

Black-Power's eyes crackled with energy and dark intent. Tope scarcely recognised him. He was heart-broken that his brother would even contemplate aggression.

"You've been with the humans too long," said Tope. He levitated, flew out and up, away from Cape Town.

## 2014

The waiter refilled his glass.

"When they reported it I was some kind of super-criminal coward. The men felt left behind, so perhaps there was some truth to it, but there were tears in my eyes," said Tope.

"Because you were brothers," said Elizabeth.

"Yes." He paused. "He looked so ridiculous in that fucking cape."

"It was kind of stupid, wasn't it?"

They both burst into laughter, loud brays of it which startled the other patrons and drew frowns from the genteel waiters.

"So what did you do?"

"Do? You know what I did. I made a costume of my own and fought back."

# SIX

**2014**

Black Power wrapped his cape around him, feeling all the more fearsome for it.

The two men facing him didn't take their cues, one clicking the safety off his pistol, the other steadying his automatic rifle.

He waved Thembeka behind him, so that she was completely hidden behind his massive bulk.

"Please let me through," he asked politely.

"Or what –?" laughed the man with the loaded pistol.

Black Power hit them both with the same punch, a left hook he'd once taught Joe Frazier, drilling both men into the wall with sickening thuds.

With a further flamboyant flourish he kicked open the barricaded door, bursting it into flying shrapnel shards of wood that burst from his foot.

People turned and gawped at them from inside the large hangar, mostly busy carrying loads of chemicals between vats; several men swung automatic rifles towards them.

*Six men, to be precise*, thought Black Power dryly, before exploding into action.

He took all six men out of action in less than thirty seconds.

The seventeen other persons had dropped what they were doing and cowered against the far wall.

"Too easy," he muttered. "*I need a real test…* I need the Pan-African."

Lost in thought, he'd failed to notice a large man enter the room through a door opposite them, a Rocket Propelled Grenade launcher on his left shoulder, locked and loaded.

48

He swung around, but it was too late.

The man fell and curled over, dead. The RPG launcher bounced once on the floor, but did not explode.

Slowly, Black Power turned to the woman standing next to him, who was lowering a pistol she had picked up earlier.

"I find the heart an easier target than the head," said Thembeka.

Black Power felt his own heart lurch a little, his head no longer lost in a forthcoming duel with Pan-African.

Or, indeed, quite so full of that smooth, beautiful interviewer he'd recognised of old, Elizabeth Kokoro.

"Let's call the drugs and toxicology units in," Thembeka said.

Black Power felt his rage grow, as he wandered along shelves bubbling with fluids fuelled by caskets of rat poison, methamphetamine and boxes of anti-retroviral medication.

Pan-African was wrong. He has helped – and could still help – this world to be a better place.

Like he had; back in '76.

## 1976

He had not predicted the death of Hector Pieterson. Indeed, June 16th had come as a huge shock to him. His contacts had warned of growing discontentment from many, but his contacts were mature men, out of touch with the youngsters of today and the real levels of rage.

Furious youngsters these were, who did <u>not</u> want to learn the language of the oppressor, Afrikaans.

Soon enough on that day, their youthful protests had turned into smoke, teargas, bullets and blood.

Black Power stood sombrely on a field nearby, watching, as a unit of the South African Defence Force gathered with a fleet of military vehicles. They had been called in to support the police, who were running, shooting and *sjambokking* youngsters further away, just outside Phefeni Junior Secondary School in Soweto, their actions misted by teargas and smoke from many fires.

The screams of the schoolchildren had already curdled his blood enough. It took all of his immense will to stop himself launching into the police to halt the mayhem.

A brigadier was briefing his troops.

This, he could stop.

With a few giant strides he was almost amongst them.

Rifles clattered, raised.

The brigadier, moustached and with thick sideburns, turned to face him with a pallid face, "You will not stop us, Black Power."

Black Power spat on the ground in front of him. "You will not do any more. The police have done more than enough."

The brigadier gave a thin smile and waved to the ranks, which parted.

A man stepped through, close to seven foot of rippling muscle and sinew, his bare and naked chest like a pinkish barrel above his camouflaged trousers and brown leather boots. Tattooed in black on his chest were the words: 'Super-Boer'.

He was blond and bland, a giant of a man who would have made Hitler proud.

The brigadier snickered: 'We have bred our own super-hero, with the right balance of steroids and hormones. Super-Boer can lift a car, you know."

"Oh," said Black Power, "Well, I can lift a fucking mountain."

He hit the blond giant then, a right jab into the midriff.

The man's breath escaped in a long whooosshhh of pain and he slowly crumpled in on himself, as his breath almost deserted his body.

Black Power knew he would not get up.

"This stops now," he said.

The brigadier stepped back as rifles were levelled at Black Power behind him.

Black Power flicked his cape in readiness.

Smoke and fading screams drifted across them. Black Power felt his eyes sting, but kept his gaze steady, his body poised to fight.

The brigadier coughed into a handkerchief, "Okay, okay, you win. We will call off this particular operation, but..."

Black Power waited tensely for the condition.

"...You will consider a sum to keep yourself in check."

"You will pay me not to act?"

"*Sekerlik*," the man said, swallowing, "For sure."

Black Power hesitated. Perhaps now was the time to sweep aside the last bastion of colonialism, allied as it was to a particularly ugly ideological racism.

But *that* bloodshed would be huge indeed.

He could conceivably do more, quietly, behind the scenes.

"Private untraceable anonymised account," he said, feeling sick and as if he'd sold his soul to Satan.

The troops were heading back to their vehicles.

Black Power turned to race across the field to help the injured and dying schoolchildren.

He had surely stopped a complete and final bloodbath.

But at what cost?

'Tope would never let me hear the end of this, should he know about this deal,' he mused, cradling a young girl's head, feeling for a pulse.

There was none.

He choked.

Tope must *never* find out.

But as for the Soweto uprising, this was only just the beginning...

And black power became the call, eventually finding a fatal focus in Steve Bantu Biko.

*As for me*, he thought, as he drifted through the decades back to the present, *I remain enduringly alive and increasingly tired of living.*

## 2014

Detective Sipho Cele scrolled through pictures of Elizabeth Kokoro on his phone.

He found them interesting, captivating, a distraction from work and his incessant pain.

They'd cleaned out the Super-Tik factory, but four more had spawned subsequently.

*The work of a super-hero is never done*, he thought absently, marvelling at how well Kokoro had aged over the decades.

He was suddenly aware of Thembeka standing behind him. "She's not bad looking for an old bitch," she said.

Sipho swivelled and scowled in his chair.

"It's not what you think," he said.

She laughed and went back to her desk. "So what am I thinking then, detective?"

For a moment he toyed with teasing thoughts out of her, he knew Tope as Pan-African had developed his own talents along those lines, very well indeed.

"Okay," he said, "I have no idea what you are thinking."

But to himself, he thought, *Brother*, (with a sudden chill of recognition and fear), *Are we to be the death of each other?*

Thembeka studied Black Power from across the room, rustling the papers in front of her PC. Deep inside her, she felt the faintest stirrings of an ancient ancestral power – but not enough to allow her to unmask his thoughts.

# SEVEN

Tope could not sleep. It wasn't that he wasn't tired, and it was not insomnia *per se*. He was sleepy. Elizabeth Kokoro's mind was too noisy for him to get any rest.

She lay naked beside him, on his left, tangled in the sheets, one breast visible like a Renaissance painting, chest rising and falling with predictable regularity. She looked peaceful.

He could not hear her breathing over the hum of the air conditioner. He idly wondered if she was a millionaire. She did not have a room; she had a suite. Maybe the cable company paid, or one of the husbands.

Incoherent nonsense leaked out of her in spurts. Fragments from blogs, tweets, status updates, junk mail headings. It was as if her brain was a web browser.

*Ben changed status to it's complicated.*

*Pictures of my cat.*

*Ope's thanksgiving photos!*

*Anselem liked your post!*

Banal, banal, banal! Why was this shit on her mind? She must spend hours surfing the net, looking for news stories.

The lovemaking had been surprising, tender. Given her sharp edges he had expected harshness, vigour, pain even. But no. She liked to be held softly and kissed, although she did not resist Flaubert's suppleness and corruption.

His phone beeped. It was Bank.

*Shall I pack? Are we still leaving tomorrow?*

Tope stole a glance at Elizabeth's nipple.

*Call the desk. Book an extra day.*

## 1975
## Lagos, Nigeria.

Tope wandered around the fabric sellers in Idumota, sometimes slipping between adjacent Molue buses. He searched for a suitable length of *Ankara* cloth.

He needed something durable. Some of the less savoury sellers soaked the fabric in starch so that it seemed stiff. One wash and it would degrade right before your eyes.

When he found what he wanted he haggled and traded insults with the seller. An onlooker would think it was a family squabble, not a transaction. Once the settled on a price, they became best friends and swore eternal fealty for sixteen generations.

Then he hopped on a bus and visited the more upmarket Kingsway and UTC general stores to find a diving suit. Not easy since scuba diving was not a serious pastime in Nigeria, but he found something next to a vicious harpoon gun. The shop assistant said they sold more of the gun than the suits.

It was late so he took a taxi back to his flat in Fola Agoro. On the centre table he had a pencil sketch of a costume completed earlier. He would be everything Black Power was not. He had that black mask that covered his head with a slit for eyes and an opening for nose and mouth. Tope would not have a mask. He ground up charcoal in a mortar with a pestle and mixed it with Vaseline. This he smeared around his eyes and part of his forehead in an irregular jagged shape. Using a manual Singer sewing machine which he had owned since 1969 he sewed the fabric into a *dashiki*. He cut up the diving suit and wore the bottom half as tights.

He would not have a cape. Fuck Black Power.

He would not have boots like Black Power. He would go barefoot. Like an African. A Pan-African. *The* Pan-African.

He liked the name. It fit his political ideas.

He stood in front of the full length mirror.

*Shit, I look ridiculous too.*

## 2014

"What are you thinking?" asked Elizabeth, snapping him back to the present. She sat up in bed and left her bosom in full view.

He went to the bed and kissed her. Elizabeth's arms came up, circled his neck, drew him closer still. The flow of internet detritus stopped abruptly.

He broke the kiss. "You want to know what's cooler than a waterbed?"

She raised her eyebrows.

He levitated them both above the bed.

Soon, they were kissing again.

## 1976
## Bol, Chad.

*My God, he's fast.*

The Pan-African barely dodged the fifth punch in Black Power's flurry of blows. There was an earthquake in his skull. An earthquake with pretty lights dancing across his vision.

The wind and the rain confused him. All Tope could see was grey skies and sheets of water coming into his eyes. Water and the fists of his brother. He was spinning and could not tell which way was up.

Black Power could not fly, and was not holding on to the Pan-African. How the hell was he in the air so much? He was gone again. Tope tried to orient himself. There was a crack of thunder and impact. Black-Power was back, digging body shots at the Pan-African's belly. He was seeing black dots. What?

*Shit, am I losing consciousness?*

It was his ambush. He was supposed to have the advantage of surprise. Black Power had recovered so quickly, surprise meant nothing.

Headshot. The whole world shook. Even the rain drops fucking shook. Pan-African had to get away. Lake Chad was somewhere, above or below.

*Fly away. Pick a direction and fly away. The direction doesn't matter. He'll kill you.*

Fuck, fuck, fuck.

He flew, fast as he could manage, the direction of his head. He knew he was moving, but the wind was so powerful that he couldn't tell where he was. The horizon was gone. No reference point. He heard a thump, and he knew that meant Black Power had taken one of his powerful leaps. The Pan-African directed himself away from the sound. He tried to take a breath, but it was mostly water and he coughed. His *dashiki* was tattered.

*Fly above the storm.*

He spat, and the blood-stained phlegm hit him right in the face.

He felt a separate rush of air and a black cloth. The sonovabitch missed him by inches and fell back to Earth. He stuck his right middle finger out at the Pan-African as he fell.

Tope flew the other way, into the clouds.

## 2014

Tope took a sip of the fresh orange juice Elizabeth offered.

"Well!" said Elizabeth. She was swaddled in the hotel's white fluffy bathrobe.

"What?"

"That was new."

"I bet you say that to all the boys."

"I'm serious."

"I'm hungry."

Elizabeth shoved a butter croissant in his general direction and poured more juice. She handed him the glass and drank straight from the jar. Room service had delivered two glasses but they had smashed one in a bout of passion.

"You surf the net a lot," said Tope.

"What do you mean? Have you been reading my mind again?"

"Not intentionally. You leaked stuff. Nothing organised, but it kept me awake. All of it was web shit."

"It's a long story. I'm... well, I'm sort of plugged into the web."

A phrase popped into her head, *web witch*, but Tope did not know what it meant. He was about to ask, but her phone rang. She had a Fela ringtone. He knew the song: *Zombie*. Not about the undead, but the soldiers who obey orders without question.

Elizabeth nodded, hummed, hemmed and hawed. "I'll get back to you."

"Who was that?"

"Do you know Lekan Deniran?"

"No."

"He's the biggest promoter in the country, some say on the continent."

"Look at my face. This is my impressed expression. Notice how similar it is to my don't-give-a-shit expression. What does he want from you?"

"Not me. You." She tied a strip of cloth around her hair.

"And?"

"He wants to promote a fight between you and Black Power."

# EIGHT

**15,000 B.P.**

The elder watched his younger brother stride off to the North, with heavy heart.

*Will I see you again, brother?* he thought to himself. *Be safe – and stay good.*

He half hoped his brother could pick up his slightly guarded sentiment, but within mere moments he was gone from view, hidden under a forest canopy.

The small group of primates they had witnessed together, returning from a hunt, were gathered around their injured one. The primate was clasping at blood dripping from a red hole amongst his left set of ribs, slowly stumbling to his hands and knees.

The elder – he decided to call himself Umvelinqangi then – watched, with some dispassionate interest, as the group gathered around their stricken group member, now panting his distress into the stubby grasslands.

The largest male amongst them was carrying a squat warthog, oozing serous fluids down his broad back.

Two of the healthy primates picked up short stabbing spears, red from their hunt.

What would it be? Stabbing – or stabbing and eating?

Umvelinqangi caught a flurry of sub-linguistic neural activity, watching postures shift with fluid non-verbal communications; a nod here, a grunt there.

The primates lowered the spears under their injured one's arms and chest at the front, pelvic region at the back. Another group member stepped forward and with forest vine, secured the hafts of the spear to arms and legs.

Four of them shifted to grasp the ends of the spears and hoisted their injured one into the air.

He was now slumped and unconscious, but they were taking him home. The giant with the dead warthog pointed onwards.

The hunting party of eight began their march across the grassy terrain, heading for a large cave at the foothills of the Mountains. *uKhahlamba* thought Umvelinqangi, *That shall be their name –* towering blue-tall in the distance, cloud – or perhaps even snow-capped.

Suddenly, he felt at home, more than he had ever felt in fifty thousand Earth equivalent cycles on his home planet.

With one stride he was amongst the group.

They scattered in terror, for he was much larger and more powerful than they and wearing shining fabric, as of nothing they had as yet seen.

*This primate will not last the journey, bleeding like this,* he thought, removing some healing *kenth* from a pouch on his belt. He spat onto the brown paste, rubbed it vigorously between his palms and then knelt down to apply it to the primate's broken skin, where a rib gaped through, white and ragged.

The group members were returning, hesitant, baring teeth and with raised arms threatening to stab at him with short wooden spears.

Umvelinqangi stood and spoke with a voice like thunder that made them all cower, including the giant, who had dropped the warthog in their initial scattering. "He will be well."

And, as if on cue, the primate groaned and opened his eyes.

The other primates fell to their knees, but Umvelinqangi knelt with them, heeding his own advice to his younger brother.

'I will not be a god, I will live amongst you,' he said, knowing they could not understand him.

But his old crew mates, their previous comrades, could indeed understand him, even at such a distance.

Astonished eyes turned to stare at the sleek rise of a space ship from above the distant forest canopy, but perhaps to them, it appeared nothing more than a huge glinting bird rising into the sky without wings.

*Farewell, comrades,* thought Umvelinqangi. *Give us twenty thousand cycles to set this planet on a path of consciousness.*

The ship was gone in a blink of light.

Umvelinqangi felt his hearts grow heavy again.

'We will not fail you,' he thought, 'my brother and I.'

(Somewhere, unbidden, the name 'Oduduwa' came to mind.)

Umvelinqangi gouged away marks on his cheeks with his fingernails, marks which traced their alien lineage, feeling lacings of his own blood dripping down his scarred cheeks.

*Do* not *fail me, brother,'* he thought. *For now I am become human, and we must show them the way of good.*

## 1976
## Bol, Chad

Black Power watched Pan-African streak away in the sky above, trailing an erratic spray of moisture and blood behind him.

A tropical storm brooded and flashed intermittently around him, as he cradled a bruised left forearm, feet anchored to the cracked earth waiting for the storm to spill fully.

*Bastard's strong and quick, I'll give that to him,* he thought, grudgingly.

Deep inside though, there was a wail of despair.

*Brother,* why *have you failed me?*

1976, now that was also a shit year, an *esabeka* year.

## 2014

Thembeka was persistent in her hunt for the local Super-Tik Drug-Lord.

Detective Sipho could only admire as she flung clues and tit-bits of information into her software algorithm incessantly, 'Vang-A-Dief' ©/ 'Catch-A-Thief' ©/ 'Bamba Isela ©'. He hurried over to her PC yet again as she shrieked once she had narrowed the Street Map search eventually to a lush, loaded mansion in Bishop's Court, perched luxuriously on the rump of Table Mountain.

But the Detective sensed Thembeka's drop in mood and noted her slumped shoulders as the Street Cams panned around the building, bulwarked with razor-wire, deadly electrics and black-clad men armed with heavy artillery.

"No way through that," she groaned.

"Who said anything about going through?" asked Black Power, caped and hulking at her right shoulder.

Night fell early in the Western Cape winter, aided by a dull and cloudy sky and a bitter North-Wester.

Black Power and Thembeka sat in the back of a marked Telkom van, seemingly busy with monitoring faltering electricity supplies to those few, who slurped up the most.

But as blackness fell, hardly kept at bay by flickering pallid orange street lights, they crept out of the van and Black Power embraced her protectively with his cape as she finished holstering her pistol, safety off.

"Ready?" he asked, thrilling to her close warmth, the tangy smell of a spicy perfume.

"Ready," she grinned up at him.

He braced his calves and with a light but firm bounce he was soaring over the walls and heading down towards the roof, carefully aiming for the part of the house likeliest (87.4% prediction) to hold the Drug-Lord, only known as Zumba.

They crashed through the roof with an explosive shower of tile, wood and mortar, Thembeka shrouded in Black Power's cape and arms.

He landed with a steely bracing of his booted legs on a meeting room table, crashing through to the marble floor below.

Debris clattered down around them as Black Power swept the remnants of the table away and Thembeka spun and unfurled from his cape across the floor, pistol cocked, sliding on her knees, trying to find a target.

Automatic fire opened up at the imposing target of Black Power. He laughed then, a booming, bursting laugh that dropped the remains of the roof on top of them all; the eight gunmen stopped shooting, confused.

There was a man standing quietly amongst his bodyguards, empty handed and purple satin suited. A small man, who broke into a sudden spin, pirouetting like flickering lightning across empty space, seizing Thembeka with a left arm around the throat from behind. He hauled her to her feet, a human shield in front of Black Power, knife in his right hand at her throat.

"Super-Tik," he said, "Speeds you up. Leave – or she dies."

Black Power hesitated – and blood spilled suddenly from Thembeka's throat.

*Bang!*

The small man staggered backwards.

Thembeka had her left arm twisted behind her, her pistol wafting the barest of smoke.

Zumba dropped like a puppet without strings as Thembeka clutched at her throat frantically, staunching the blood.

With one leap, Black Power had seized her and exploded out of the house.

Landing near the van outside the mansion, Black Power burst open the back door with a forceful finger, panicking.

Inside, he laid Thembeka gently down, securing the door from the inside.

When he turned around, Thembeka was sitting up and staring at him, a soft and bemused expression on her face

Black Power noted a drying trickle of blood down the front of her throat.

"You're – okay," he croaked.

She smiled.

He leant across the floor of the van and kissed her.

Softly.

Slowly.

She slapped him.

"What was that for?" He asked, aggrieved, sure for once he had not read her signals wrong.

"That's for thinking of Kokoro while kissing me," she snapped.

He was speechless.

Thembeka stood up and pushed at the door. It buckled outwards and she jumped through the burst metal of the door.

Black Power could only stare after her.

How on earth did she know what he was thinking?

And her slap had actually – hurt!

Then a slow and ancient memory came to him. A faintest taste of something he had used up some millennia ago.

*Kenth.*

He had always marvelled at his anatomical and DNA similarities to emerging humans – life-forms on planets separated by light years, but with puzzling similar evolutionary pathways. Not completely compatible however, his sperm was infertile with humans – *perhaps just as well,* he thought to himself wryly.

His realisation was clear – Kenth had bound to the DNA of that primate he had helped heal, seventeen millennia back.

And he had kissed that man's very distant long-lost descendant.

Thembeka's thin and dormant strand of alien DNA had somehow become activated... perhaps at their first touch?

...And she had indeed read his mind.

"Thembeka, some back!" he called.

But all he could hear was the gathering sound of police sirens.

# NINE

**2014**

On the table was a scale model of a modified geodesic dome, although Tope felt sure that Buckminster Fuller never intended his invention for this purpose. Elizabeth squeezed his hand once. He glanced at her briefly, then focused his mind on what Lekan was saying.

"Titanium lattice shell with carbonised steel geodesics, non-rigid structure which will snap back after impact. One hundred thousand small cameras all around which will give spectators true 3-D, not that crap you see in the multiplexes. I plan to project the conflict into stadia worldwide."

Lekan Deniran wasn't a tall man, but he was charismatic and energetic. His eyes burned with that fever that afflicts avaricious men everywhere. He talked with a pace that accelerated when he got to the financial reward. Dark, wiry, relentless. Dressed simple in jeans and a t-shirt because, it was rumoured, he saw Donald Trump dressed like this once in *Time* magazine.

"Tell me about the kinematics of this thing," said Tope. "I don't want any bystanders getting hurt. What amount of force will this structure resist?"

"Fifty thousand pounds was the limit of testing," said Lekan.

"Is that a lot?" asked Elizabeth.

"Your high performing boxer can punch about twelve hundred pounds," said Lekan.

"Black Power is an Ubermensch, not a sportsman," said Tope.

"Do you think he can punch with more force than that?" asked Lekan.

"I don't know."

"Can you?"

"I don't know. I don't use force in that way. I don't punch with muscular strength," said Tope.

"Explain," said Elizabeth, ever the journalist.

"My powers are mental. I levitate, and that becomes flight. I lift objects. I detect thoughts. I have a limited force field around my body. When I punch what I do is push with my mind. The mass of the object should not matter, but because I see with my eyes the difference between a pebble and a boulder the effort I apply is different. I should be able to punch a hole in the moon theoretically, but my brain tells me it's impossible, so I can't."

"Can you beat him?" asked Lekan, handing drinks to them.

Tope didn't answer; a brief flash of red desert sand, snow and a twinge in his malformed arm distracted him.

Lekan shrugged. "It doesn't matter. We'll all be rich at the end of it. We stand to make a gazillion bucks domestic alone."

"How will you get him to agree to the bout?" asked Elizabeth.

Lekan hesitated. "I'm still trying to contact his people."

"Does he have people?" she asked.

"I don't know, but if he does, I'll find them." He emptied his glass and poured another. "I'm flying to South Africa tomorrow. I'll find him."

"How did you get him to the desert?" asked Elizabeth.

"I sued for peace," said Tope. "I offered a truce. I tried to appeal to his rationality by showing the futility of our enmity."

"So how did it turn to a battle?" asked Elizabeth.

"The man has no rationality."

## February 18, 1979

"This is why you brought me here?" asked Black Power. "To discuss books and the deranged theories of cocaine-addicted alienists?"

They stood apart from each other, scrub and red sand between them. Eddies carried dust in chaotic ballets.

66

"It's time for this to end," said the Pan-African. "This farce. I've been reading Berne's work. This thing between you and me, it's a game. We're playing "hero", brother."

"What is this babbling? You sound like a baboon."

"We don't really want to kill each other. I'm trying to educate you and you are trying to chastise a younger brother. Neither of us is playing for keeps. This battle will last forever, with continued attrition and no real resolution. Come the day that this sun goes nova we'll still be standing."

"You're right about one thing," said Black Power. "I am trying to chastise you. I have done so many times."

"I won't fight you this time."

"Then you'll die because I won't hold back."

"Death, then," said the Pan-African. At the time, he meant it.

## 2013

The wedding dress was off-white and the shoes scuffed, but the radiance of the bride's smile did a lot to neutralise the imperfections. The ring-bearer led her to the courtyard, a boy of nine with a solemn expression on his face. The drummers picked up a frenzied beat and barefoot dancers began their performance. The mother of the bride wailed as if someone had died. Everybody sang. A few of the older men were drunk and off-key, but nobody cared.

The bride was pregnant. Tope could hear the proto-thoughts of the growing child. She already recognised her mother's heartbeat and voice. The mother was, as yet, unaware of the life growing in her.

"So, what do you say?" asked Elizabeth Kokoro. She was irritating in the extreme.

"Miss Kokoro, you're not invited to this wedding."

"It's a lot of money."

"We shoot *mo gbo, mo ya* in these parts, you know."

"We'll get your side of the story. Finally, after all these years."

The groom danced with the little bride. Tope had bought the suit, but it didn't fit the man well. Some men wheeled in gigantic black loud speakers and started playing *juju* music. In between bowls of *jollof* rice people took to the dance floor, spraying money on each other.

"It doesn't matter to me if anyone gets to hear my side of the story. I know what happened." He took a bite out of a fried chicken thigh. He deliberately chewed with his mouth open to seem as crude as possible. He offered the drumstick to her, but she ignored it. He bit it again. "Go back to the city, girl. I'm busy here."

"With the society wedding of the century?" she said.

"Do not mock these people. They are poor, but their emotions are genuine. They have dignity."

"Ahh, good. Anger. I was starting to feel that nothing meant anything to you any more."

"God, you're like a tse-tse fly, buzzing around. Go away."

She took the drumstick from him and tore a piece of flesh, then she spoke with her mouth full. "I saw you once, you know. In Accra in '77."

Something dawned on Tope. "You took those photographs of me and Black Power fighting in the water reservoir."

"Yes."

"The first clear photos the news outlets had of me. Not very flattering, if I remember." Black Power had his boot on Tope's chest and his cape flew in the wind. It was a poster and t-shirt graphic and the second major internet meme after 'All your base are belong to us' according to Bank.

"I had to crawl through mud to get there."

"I remember you. Skinny little girl, you looked like a worm." Not really. She had looked like a snake with breasts.

"Did you hate me?"

"No, I just mildly resented you."

"Come do the TV show."

"No."

68

But Tope did.

## 2014

On the road back to the settlement, Bank shoved a screen in front of his face.

"What am I looking at?" said Tope.

"That's Black Power," said Bank.

Tope looked at the tablet and saw the tube video. Mobile phone footage of a few indistinct blurs and a shadow that might have been a cape. Maybe a sub-machine gun in the footage. A woman on the ground. A dog. *A dog?*

"This is blurry," said Tope.

"It's Black Power. He's back. Read the comments. The guy who was there saw him. It's just a few days ago."

"This is a guy in a mask and cape, Bank. He's wearing a box shirt and chinos. That was never –"

"Trust me. The interweb never lies."

"The interweb lies all the time."

"Whatev. They're bigging up your upcoming bout with him," said Bank. He snatched his tablet band and started moving his fingers around again.

"I haven't agreed to do it."

"Uncle, with that money we can bribe enough government officials to practically own the land on which we live. We won't have to go to court. You can feed people or something. Send more of us to university."

"I know."

"Then what?"

"It's cheap."

"Tens of millions of –"

"Not that kind of cheap. I mean, we're not back street pugilists." *We are gods, and we do not fight for your entertainment,* Tope thought, but he did not say aloud.

Bank said, "Do not think we are unappreciative of you, Uncle. I love you more than my father."

"Your father left before you were born. You've never met him."

"Yes, and I love you more than I love him."

"Go back to your tablet, Bank."

Tope watched the countryside go by.

"Do not let them begin to worship you" his brother had said, yet Black Power was the one who allowed it to happen first.

He felt the hair on his neck rise; Elizabeth was thinking of him. Miles away, but he could still feel her thoughts.

It was time for one last fight. In Lekan's arena they would put it to rest once and for all.

# TEN

**1800 to 1828**
**Kwa-Zulu Natal Midlands.**

The boy grew up a bastard, but Dingiswayo – as the elder allowed himself to be known then – recognised something special in that boy. As the boy became a young man, he was prone to angry outbursts to be sure, rising as he did to the frequent challenges of his fully parented peers. One day, he had even run a twelve miles return journey through thorn-tree foothills, to head off and return seven cattle from the neighbouring Langeni tribe – having silently cut the throat of one of their herders.

So, when that fiery bastard became a full man, his circumcision scars long healed, the elder gave him an ibutho lempi, his fighting regiment.

*This should channel his energies constructively*, thought the elder, saying only aloud: "Be careful with your men, Shaka, their lives and their families are in your keeping."

The young man respectfully avoided his gaze, as if indeed restrained and finally maturing, "Yes, my Chief."

But, in ongoing skirmishes with the neighbouring tribes, Shaka retained his impulsive and reckless manner, somehow knowing the best times to do so, being almost always victorious. On the death of their father, Sigujano – Shaka's half-brother – was the rightful heir to the vacant throne, but Shaka was aided by the elder, Dingiswayo, to seize military control. He was taken by surprise, however, when Shaka had his brother executed.

*How can you kill your own brother?* thought the elder, wondering as to what might be happening to his own younger brother, up North for millennia now.

71

The elder, using vestiges of his mental manipulation, eventually feigned his own murder as Dingiswayo at the hands of Zwide, the Chief from the Ndwanwe clan – and waited to see what would happen. He now observed the proceedings as Shaka's bodyguard, his own features additionally altered by the slightest of projected imaginal suggestions.

And, as months rolled into years, King Shaka shaped his people around him, the Bodyguard watching, always watching – but sometimes fighting, reining in his strength, so as not to alarm those around him too much, particularly the King.

For the King was building an empire.

Shaka had quickly stopped the initiation rights for boys to men, manhood no longer stemming from wasted strength in circumcision rites, but in active age-cohort regiments, along with training and strategy, military strategy. And weapons, new weapons – throwing spears that are lost on the battlefield, the assegais, were moved to a secondary weapon – a new short stabbing spear, an ikiwa, was adopted, alongside a bigger cowhide shield that was used offensively, after Shaka had showed the superiority of these new weapons in bloody training bouts that included some men – even friends – dying.

"From now on, a man who loses his ikiwa in battle will lose his life," said the King, as his impi warriors and empire grew rapidly. For this was the start of Mfecane, the 'crushing', the making of a mighty people who expanded into occupying a huge geographical space, absorbing many, yet leaving many others dead or fleeing into the expanses before them. Down towards the southern seas of this vast Continent…

But, thankfully, some things did not change. Still, mothers and often grandmothers, when they could, sang and recited the old tales that spoke to them all; stories about Why the Cheetah's Cheeks are Stained and even older stories from the very beginning, about how the Sky-God, Nkulunkulu, made the world and the First Man, Umvelinqangi, emerged from watery reeds with his wife, able to draw on thunder and lightning.

*I am indeed Zulu,* thought the Bodyguard elder on these good evenings, sitting nearby as the women thrilled the children with these tales, enjoying hearing his ancient name being dropped in these living tales, as well as thinking about the brutal genius of his King, who finally defeated and killed Zwide, Dingiswayo's murderer.

But in time, word came to Shaka from startled and shaken scouts, of a new people, perhaps Gods or devils, who were as white as crushed limestone. They too were moving, but moving steadily up towards the amaZulu; slowly, yet inexorably.

*Evolutionary brother primates,* thought the Bodyguard to himself, *Perhaps returning from milder climes where their melanocytes have not been so active? So brother will meet brother again at last, reunited.*

Ever looking for allies and advantage, Shaka invited some of them in.

But – the Bodyguard learned in due time – the white brothers and sisters brought firearms, disease, and not the slightest recognition of their long lost family...

As for Shaka, the Bodyguard was deployed elsewhere when his half-brothers Dingane and Mahlangana murdered him in turn.

*What is it about brothers?* thought the elder grimly, on hearing the news.

## 2014
### Strandfontein Beach

There is a place where many wild gulls breed, along a sandy cliff on the False Bay coast of the Cape Town outskirts, just past Strandfontein. The place is protected, a sanctuary for gulls to breed together and fly free, unhindered by humans, searching for fish and scatterings of white and black mussel, that they raise on high and drop, to shatter on the rocks below, exposing pale, delicate meat, ripe for the taking.

From this gull sanctuary, a man or woman, if they are tall enough, can cast their gaze inland, across the Cape Flats, where a vast expanse of informal settlements shine in the sun. Mostly shacks cobbled and jury-rigged from tin, aluminium, chipboard and wire, rainproofed with black plastic bags or sheets, some sprouting wide and circular satellite dishes. This township is home to over half a million, stitched together in districts such as Mandela Park, Tembani and Harare.

So it was that Black Power came to stand and watch; a man indeed tall enough to see much, who watched with an acute and painful vision, across that vast and chaotic spread of Khayelitsha township. This place was but one of a multitude of the enduring legacies of apartheid, some indeed now improved since liberation. This place was certainly not one of those that had been significantly improved, despite money swilling around for twenty years since the first democratic elections in South Africa. Some electrification, surely, to cast light on a dark place... but not enough light. There was indeed a good reason he had chosen mid-day.

Slowly, Black Power shook his head. He preferred to look at the inner city opulence of parts of the central metropolis – like the view from his office as Detective Cele – not at this huge broken patchwork of poverty, where Tuberculosis and the HIV virus continued to wreak their deadly havoc. It was not a good reminder, that, for all his power, he had actually achieved so little.

His – brother – had never tired of reminding him of this!

Black Power turned to look at the sea instead, an easier and more pleasant sight, where the incessant roll of surf on white sand soothed his mind, yet also somehow reminded him of how old he had become. Perhaps he should just head home; it was a Saturday after all, or he could catch a movie at the Waterfront, the new Tarantino film was supposed to be brilliant.

Alone. He would be alone.

Clenching his fist, he looked down at the ripple of muscle along his wrist, underneath his black kevlar-laced glove. He was Black Power for fuck's sake, he had stopped volcanoes and faced whirlwinds, he could handle one little paltry... visit.

Steeled, he turned to face the sparkling sea of shiny shacks, alien vision searching for the small bricked day hospital far in the distance, at the locale of Site C, Khayelitsha.

There. Got it. Shit, that's quite some distance, out on the far distant extreme range of his jumps.

But he knew that if he took a slower or more mundane way in, a taxi or bus, his commitment would falter and he would change his route, heading home – or anywhere else. However, the shacks were so densely packed, there was no way he could risk taking more than one jump.

There, that field, next to the hospital, was dusty and open, uninhabited.

Good training too, should he ever need to face his brother again.

Come on, focus, bend, brace... No! Not enough purchase here, the sand was shifting beneath his bulk, sliding away under his boots. Perhaps he could have done this in the seventies.

Not now, his stomach was no longer quite so taut, his muscles did not sing quite so beautifully to him, with their clear sense of invulnerable power. So, with one small step, Black Power bounced onto the empty beach road, legs together, recoil... and JUMP!

He hurtled high into the air like a homing missile, exhilarated by the wind-whistle of his passage and the warm cross-wind buffeting of a berg breeze drifting down from the Mountain. Below him, shacks blurred together in a moving chaotic collage, growing clearer, larger and more distinct as he headed back to earth.

He was heading to the centre of the field near the hospital, his aim indeed true.

But now he could see some boys, six or seven of them, playing football with a small stack of positioned bricks marking their goals, scuffing sand as they chased the ball in the middle of the field.

"No!!!!!!" he shouted, but the wind whipped his words over his shoulders and up into the sky, as he dropped like a lethal boulder.

One boy looked up and shouted, pointing.

"Is it a bird?" he thought he heard in isiXhosa and then he was dropping onto the stationery boy, whose mouth was gawping wide in sudden frozen shock.

Khayelitsha!

Black Power landed on one foot, his second leg raised to avoid contact with the cowering boy, pushing away desperately to avoid impact. Sand and dirt exploded from the impact of his landing, showering the boy, as he bounced and rolled away, impelled by the forceful, juddering impetus of his left leg.

Black Power finally rolled to a halt. *Shit*, he thought, *I'm tangled in my fucking cape – and my leg hurts like hell.*

He lay for some moments, trying to catch his breath.

The young boy stood over him, unhurt but sandy, holding a football. "Mister, can you be a referee for us, please?"

Black Power unleashed a string of invectives in isiZulu, but he knew the boy would understand; they were cousin languages after all, united by the Mfecane. Slowly, he unrolled himself from his cape and sat up.

The field was now deserted.

Sighing with sudden guilt, he stood up gingerly, testing his left leg.

Fine. A bit sore, but it would pass. *Not good news for you, my brother,* he thought to himself, his gaze tracing a route from the hospital to a mixed spread of brick houses and shacks, some flattened for redevelopment.

There. That was the address. A small brick house just off the bend in the road feeding the hospital, he recognised it from an earlier zoom-in on Google Earth.

*Modest, but better than many other abodes here,* he thought, making his way towards the house, walking off his slight limp.

A small crowd had gathered on the outskirts of the field, whispering together, gazing at him in awe.

"I told you Black Power was back," he heard one voice clearly amongst the clamour.

There were other voices, other words... and, and that FUCKING word again! Even after so many years, it still ripped deep into his being.

He had reached the road by then, the crowd parting before him like the Red Sea to Moses, but he turned and roared: "For the record, I was never an... an... Askari!" He spat the word so they could see his contempt. "I never betrayed the Struggle... Amandla!"

He raised his fist.

There was silence.

"Amandla!" he shouted again, louder, more urgent.

"Ngawethu," came a soft reply, from an older voice hidden amongst the crowd.

'Born Frees!' he sighed with exasperation and, suddenly feeling slightly foolish, he turned on his heels.

Thembeka was standing in front of him, fists on either side of a broad hipped black skirt, her red T-shirt etched with a slogan in black – 'Pissed Off Woman.'

"Oh –" he took a step backwards. There was no need for her to be so literal.

"Why couldn't you have just come quietly and knocked on the door?"

"Uh –"

"My God, but you're inarticulate, even for a man."

"Sorry," he looked down at his dusty boots, feeling a rush of blood to his face and the faster pattering of his hearts.

She smiled then, even if it was gone in a flash.

"So," she said, fists now off her hips, hands opened wide, "Why have you come to see me then?"

A full taxi hooted, on its way to nearby Mitchells Plain.

They stepped quickly off the road, but an older man was hurrying up to them, holding up a shiny object.

"Eh –?" said Black Power.

Thembeka burst out laughing.

It was an old comic book, glinting in a protective plastic cover. An early 'Black Power' comic from '75 that he recognised, with his first face-off against Pan-African and an Angolan war back-story, pointing out the evils of the communist take over by the MPLA.

"Would you mind signing this for me, Black Power?" burbled the man, "It's in Near Mint condition." The man was dressed in orange council overalls, perhaps a foreman in one of their service departments.

"How much would it be worth then?" Black Power asked.

The man shrugged awkwardly and Black Power could tell by his lined faced and greying hair he was probably upwards of fifty years old.

He took the offered pen and the opened comic book, braced against its protective backing board, that had been part of the sealed package. The pen hovered over the opening splash page with its writing credits. Black Power looked sharply at the waiting man, who stood, openly holding his breath.

"So," said Black Power, "What do you think of my role in the Struggle?"

The man looked him in the eyes. "You should be recognised as a Struggle hero, because you challenged the apartheid regime every step of the way. And you only held back from a direct and open confrontation, in order to save many more lives."

Black Power smiled. "So, to whom should I dedicate this to?"

## Strandfontein Beach

The surf pounded to his left, but they were alone. This stretch of the beach – between Monwabisi and the Strandfontein sewerage outlet – was often deserted, apart from the odd lone fisherman, but it was clearly deserted now.

Still, Black Power had never been a man of many words. He had even forgotten the alien language of his birth, only remembering faint echoes of no longer familiar sounds, loosely linked to vague images and objects; smells that tantalised him, that he could no longer name, a black sky – and a red sun.

"So?" she said expectantly, hands on hips again, "What is happening to me? Why am I gaining these powers?"

He splayed his hands open to her, with a gesture of helpless ignorance. "My best guess is you may have tracings of an – er, ancestor of mine's DNA, which has become activated in the presence of my own powers."

"Oh." She looked down at the beach sand, kicking with her bare right foot at a brown piece of kelp. The kelp shot out over the furthest breaking wave. She looked up again, "Can you take these powers back?"

Slowly, he shook his head, aware she could read his mind anyway.

She turned away and he could tell from the slight shaking of her shoulders, she was crying.

He went over to her and touched her left shoulder gently. "I feel like such a freak," her words warbled back to him, from over her shoulder.

"Thembeka," he said, "I've always felt a freak."

She turned then and gave him a soft smile, "I'm sorry." Her arms were open, inviting.

He stepped forwards and embraced her.

Lovingly.

"Detective," she said sharply, "I can feel your – interest – and right now, I don't share it!"

He smiled into the nape of her neck. "That's okay, love," he said, "I've got more than enough interest for the both of us."

She kneed him hard…

…and her aim was true.

Slowly, and with much unfamiliar pain, he folded in on himself, until he was curled in a foetal position on the soft sand, clutching his deeply burning – now flaccid – penis and testicles.

She stood over him, legs astride, and he could feel the heat of her rage. "No means fucking N-O, okay? We've had enough of rape, corrective or otherwise, get it?"

He lifted his head to look up at her.

Coldness grasped his hearts. He could see a distant look in her eyes, as if he no longer existed to her.

"Sala kahle," she said, "Goodbye, Detective."

She looked up at the sun, as if concentrating and... flew.

He sat up, but she had gone, the gulls wheeling and screeching in her wake.

And, with a sudden aching realisation that made the pain in his privates feel trivial, he became aware that she would not come back.

Gone.

Like everyone does, eventually.

Gone.

Alone again.

Thembeka had flown off, just like Pan-Fucking-African.

He pulled a cell-phone out of a small utility clip in his cape. "I've got more surprises than you'll like in this cape that you dared mock, brother!" He barked at the crashing waves.

Two calls.

One, to request a transfer to Johannesburg.

Jozi -- where it's really happening! A real African city, not like this effete Europeanised pretender...

Two, to Phulani, AKA the Sharp, Sharp Fixer.

"Get me Pan-African," he said, "Any way you can."

Time to end this, brother.

Finally, once and for all time.

# ELEVEN

**1978**
**Lagos, Nigeria.**

Space.

He was not really here. This was a memory or a dream. Hanging there was a space station, spiky, crystalline almost. The hull was grown by a layer of bacteria genetically modified to produce the bulkhead. It was constantly sheared off and constantly regrown. Inside, there were hundreds of individuals. Tope was once there. Sleeping for millennia, aeons, time unmeasurable in Earth terms.

The memory wavers, then there is a skiff, broken off from the space station, a needle, with dozens on board. A blue planet. Beautiful. Atmospheric. The needle breaches the atmosphere, shatters and the people scatter into different areas of the landmass. Tope and his brother land in what will be known as Africa. They land, steaming and smoking from the heat of re-entry.

Tope woke up.

At first he did not know where he was. There were empty Guilder bottles all around him, brown, broken, some half-full. His bottom felt cold and at first he felt he had wet himself, but no, it was the cold of concrete.

He had a headache and the world seemed too bright.

"Pan-African, stay where you are!"

A loud voice projected by a megaphone. Stern. Loud. Did it have to be so loud?

He waved the voice away and tried to open his eyes again. Tope was in the centre of a crater. This was about a foot deep, fifty yards wide. Cracked rocks radiated away from him. The blackened carcass of a twisted bicycle smoked close by.

*What?*

He could not remember the night before. There was spent ordnance all around. He felt his body-nothing damaged. His force field always kicked in when he was unconscious.

God, he needed a piss.

He pulled down his Y-fronts and urinated, a long satisfying, steaming stream of yellow. Then he realised he was surrounded by the Nigerian army.

*Ah, hence the debris and shells.*

"Halt!"

"Please, I beg you, stop shouting," said Tope. "I have a hangover."

A shot rang out and others joined in. Tope's force field stopped the urine and the reflux caused pain to shoot up his pelvis. The bullets also managed to buffet him about. His head throbbed. *Oh, God. Why won't they leave me alone? What did I ever do to deserve this?*

He flew straight up into the sky. At a hundred feet he pissed over all of them.

"Golden shower, assholes!" He shook himself off and giggled. Maybe he was still a bit drunk. Fragments of the night before came back.

From the height he could see the devastation. The crater he woke up in was the tail end of a three-mile serpentine path of destruction which included broken shops, ruptured roads, twisted median strip railings, upturned cars, concertinaed lorries, uprooted street lights (they didn't work anyway!), snapped palm trees, downed power lines, cracked buildings, shattered glass, and clumps of... smouldering matter that he hoped to God were not the remains of human beings.

Fuck.

There were sawhorses and barricades keeping people at bay, and the army was in position with tanks, armoured vehicles and a mounted multiple rocket launcher.

They fired up at him. He flew higher, then away. Had he done that? He had seen the Nigerian Army use a scorched earth approach in Obalende during the attempted coup in 1976. Tope could remember flattening the trucks. He got flashes of violence and laughter. Smiling lissom women. Booze. More booze. Music. Orlando Owo and Victor Uwaifo. Trumpets and guitars. Groovy!

He came down in Oworonsoki, near the Lagos Lagoon. Mostly unpaved streets with pools of relentless mud. Low-income residential area. Barefoot children. He staggered, swayed, and vomited into the stagnant water of the open gutters, disturbing the mosquito larvae as they incubated. A Danfo bus thundered by, spraying him with red mud. He attempted to be angry, but his headache was too severe. He giggled instead.

It was mid-morning and school children in primary colours stared at him as they went to seek an education. He stumbled along to a street called Kiniun-Ifa, and he heard Akpala music come from a kind of grotto. A hand was painted on the wall to the left of the door. An open eye-ball with crude lines spiking away from it lay on the palm. The fingers were all the same size, including the thumb, and they all pointed upwards.

Tope went in.

"*Eka'abo*," said an old man. Welcome. He was seated on the floor on a raffia mat, holding a necklace. He gestured to the mat.

Tope sat opposite him. He handed Tope a gourd of water, which went down in almost one gulp. A woman came with food, as if they were expecting him. Which, of course they were. The old man was an oracle, one of the real ones. It wasn't magic; some people were just better plugged into the quantum nature of time. If time was occurring all the time, all moments at once, then travel or prophecy was theoretically possible.

Tope asked to wash, and they led him to a backyard where a pail of water, a plastic bowl, a raffia sponge and *ose okpa* (locally made soap) waited on a sheet of corrugated tin. He took off his clothes and soaped himself. The water was cold, but he didn't mind.

He returned to the first chamber when he was done. He noticed for the first time a shrine off to the left, an earthenware alcove with a lit candle illuminating an information leaflet from W.H.O about smallpox immunisation and a statuette of Sopana, the Yoruba god of smallpox. With the eradication of smallpox from Nigeria this was effectively a dead god.

The old man said some incantations over his necklace, and then held it between clasped hands.

"*Ifa olokun, a s'oro d'ayo*," the man said. "Blow."

Tope blew over his hands, feeling like a magician's assistant.

The old man threw the necklace to the mat and peered at it. He shook his head.

"What?" asked Tope.

"*Iku*," said the old man. "Death."

## 2014

"Tell me about your childhood," said Elizabeth.

"I don't remember it," said Tope.

"Any of it?"

"That's right."

"Does that seem odd to you?"

"It does. I don't think Black Power remembers either. I wonder if we were just created like this, or grown in a vat somewhere and then activated. Or perhaps we had our memories wiped."

"Let me send a car for you."

"..."

"Come on," said Elizabeth.

"I'm in the middle of something."

"With what?"

"I'm writing something," said Tope.

"What a coincidence. So am I. What are you writing?"

He was writing a will, but he did not tell her. Instead he closed the chat window, intending to lie to her about a power failure. His phone rang immediately and it was her so he ignored it.

Tope did not have family among the humans, neither did he have any real money to speak of, but if the bout went ahead he would be rich, or rich and dead. He looked out of his window and saw the settlement. He had virtually built the whole place by hand. A young girl bounced by, revelling in her new pubertal body, a girl Tope had seen squalling and smeared with meconium on the day she was born. Her mother had died, but she had been adopted by the entire settlement. The government had not succeeded in kicking them out and Bank was right. With money they could buy a fucking ministry.

The bout would happen. Lekan had called and was spreading cash around Jo'burg. "No results yet. These motherfuckers are tight-lipped, but there's some guy here or around here called Fulani or something. He may know something. I'm meeting with someone who knows his second cousin tomorrow."

And so on.

He seemed to take for granted that Tope would fight.

## February 18, 1979
## Sahara Desert

"Fight me, you bastard," said Black Power.

He smashed into the Pan-African with his right fist while holding him with the left.

Grains of sand rose off the desert floor with each hit, but the Pan-African's force field held fast. He felt no direct pain, but somewhere in his brain he felt weaker.

"I'm not afraid to die, Dingiswayo," said the Pan-African. "Are you?"

Black-Power head-butted him on the nose.

It got through.

And hurt.

# TWELVE

2014
## Radium BeerHall, Johannesburg

Jozi, Jo'burg, Johannesburg, iGoli, City of Gold…

Your golden heart is eaten out, surrounded as you are now by huge piles of empty mine debris, smaller splashes of barricaded plushness, and far vaster brooding settlements of cheap brick and shantytown settlements. But, despite the emptying of your beating heart, you continue to burn, to throb…

Detective Cele, AKA Black Power was eGoli and at rest, with a pint of the finest Charles Glass has to offer – although Phaswane Mpe had expressed this state of being far more eloquently, when he was alive and welcoming people to the Jo'burg suburb of Hillbrow.

He was slumped in his old favourite beer-hall from the 1930s – although then he had to put up with drinking in a back-door shebeen section, apartheid well on its way, even before the Nats got to power in '48. He'd even put on his old brown trilby hat from the 50s, sharp end crammed low onto his forehead, dark coat – Wesley Snipes 'Blade' style – draped over his formidable bulk.

Still, he was indeed at rest, albeit grudgingly nursing his beer, because alcohol – like so many of the viruses and bacteria around him – had limited impact on his physiology. He envied those who lost control of their speech and functions as they drank constantly, gradually slurping their way into oblivion.

Like the young white man sitting opposite him, who was seemingly not frightened by his bulk – or his silence. The

86

immediate seats around them in the Radium Beerhall were empty, as if people could sense his brooding, fragile peace.

The Detective was trying to work out whether the man, apparently Colin Jordaan, was seeking a payoff of companionship or sex.

"So they left me," said Colin, drooping into his emptied beer mug, "and I got no fucking idea why."

Perhaps he's looking for a shrink? The Detective, as always, decided to cut to the chase.

"Man or woman?" he asked.

"Eh –?" the young man lifted his long orange curls out of his mug, "Uhhhh... Joey's a... dude."

Maybe sex then. The Detective smiled to himself. He'd enjoyed a number of male encounters down the decades, but he had been forced to rein in that side of himself – he had an image to maintain, after all.

He patted Colin's hand gently, but the man still winced through his drunken stupor.

As Black Power, the Detective had been attacked by the gender brigade in the past for not embracing more sexual ambiguity and variety, especially in the light of declared Gender Wars and violence. As always, somehow he found himself on what felt like the wrong side, trying to straddle a fence that was impossible to balance on, despite all of his super-powers.

And he knew – from long history – that culture was certainly not set in stone.

Tope – the Pan-African's comments has always hurt, when he challenged his asserted umZulu identity – for Cele sensed the truth in this, although he did not want to face the void of identity as to who he really was, underneath the suit and mask...

Brother, yes, maybe a long time ago. So long ago he had no recall of any mother or father, he seemed to have been born old and almost eternal.

The Detective had a sudden impulse to whip off his dark overcoat to reveal his Black Power suit, to don his mask -- and to pick up this young man and walk past gasping patrons of this restaurant-pub, who would be snapping away at him with cell-cameras.

A pudgy, dark and greying man, suited in tribal Afro-Amani chic, shoved the drunken youth off his chair.

The young man could only say 'shitttt...' before falling in a complaining heap on the floor. He had enough control, however, to lever himself up onto a chair in the next table, glowering his discontent.

He was not noticed, the Detective and the suit crouching over their Castles, mumbling.

"You're looking older, Phulani," observed the Detective, with the eye of one who misses little.

"And you're fucking not..." scowled the pudgy man, wrinkled and grey, with the air of a man who had seen everything under the sun.

"So," said the Detective, "What news?"

"Pan African," said the old man slowly, "Wants one last bout. A final decider. To the death, winner takes all."

The Detective rocked back on the couch, which creaked its protest at his 200 kay g's and almost 7 foot of mass. "Really? What's his conditions?"

Phulani looked around the Beerhall slowly and then leaned forward. "We've got to wait for – wait for it, Lekan Deniran."

The Detective stroked his chin, smiled, "Ah, the huge fight promoter – Pan-African always did aim big."

He hauled out his phone and opened his messages, but there were none – still – from Thendeka, his phone seemingly blocked to her.

He tapped in a message and sent, but nothing seemed to happen. Cursing, he threw it across the Hall, where it clattered in a sprinkle of glass through a closed window.

"Fine," he said, "What time did you set? Is he late?"

A small, dark wiry man stood there expectantly, in jeans and a District 9 T-shirt, with the 'No Humans Allowed' sign and a shambling alien that looked like a Parktown Prawn from the movie emblazoned across his chest.

Phulani stood up and shook hands, "Cute T-shirt, Mr. Deniran."

The wiry man smiled and sat smoothly, as if accustomed to cutting to many chases. "Thank you, Fulani, I take it this big man is Black Power, in subtle disguise?"

"Phulani, the 'ph' is pronounced like a pee," said Phulani, with creased brows, "Nice T-shirt as I said – what were you, a Blomkamp extra?"

Lekan Deniran laughed, openly and genuinely, "Nollywood would have done a much better job, Phulani, but let's get to the real business at hand, shall we?"

The man turned and focused his intent gaze on the Detective; Black Power could almost see the yen signs rolling across the small man's eyeballs. "So, what are your terms and conditions, Mister Black Power?"

"I'll fight him any which way I can, in a booth
in fucking Tafawa Balewa Square, if I have to."

"Good," smiled Lekan, hauling out a tablet, "There's a contract template on here – what are your conditions."

"One mill, US dee's, here…" The Detective handed over a small square piece of paper.

Lekan looked at the paper and laughed. "Very generous, to allocate all of this to your old and ailing ex-president's charity, ex-prisoner 46664."

For some reason I have an affinity with prisoners," said the Detective, signing with an e-pen.

With a nod and a wink, Lekan slipped the tablet into his leather bag and was gone.

"What about my payment?" asked Phulani.

"The usual," said the Detective tersely.

"Oh – can you beat him?" asked Phulani boldly, "Can you beat Pan-African, once and for all?"

The Detective stood up, whipping his hat and coat off and – in full regalia, once he'd flicked his cape open and donned his mask – he bent down and kissed the very surprised, drunken white youth at the next table.

Phulani howled his outrage as cameras began to snap across the hall.

Nothing like the scent of death to focus the mind...

Thud! The young man had flung a drunken upper-cut against Black Power's chin. Power, stood up, surprised, the punch had tickled, but he'd felt it.

"Just because I'm gay doesn't mean it's all about sex," said the young man, "We're all just *people*, you know."

*Humans!* Who could understand them?

Phulani slipped a phone into Power's coat pocket and pulled at his arm, "Let's roll," he said, "bigger fish to fry."

Now *fish* he could understand!

# THIRTEEN

**February 18, 1979**
**Sahara Desert, Africa**

Black Power slammed him into the side of a mountain. There was a brief rock fall and a tumescence of dust but before the Pan-African could cough there was that grip on the scruff of his neck and... g-forces. Flung into the sky.

The rush of air, the blue sky...

The cold rouses him.

*It's beautiful up here.*

Impact. A light brighter than the sun, then darkness. He woke, then two seconds later he hit the desert ground.

Black Power landed after him with a heavy vibration. He grabbed the Pan-African's right arm and spun him like a centrifuge, clockwise, then after a half-turn he stopped, then turned counter-clockwise.

The Pan-African's body was still moving clockwise and the bones popped like cheap fireworks. His scream echoed and the involuntary psychic feedback immobilised Black Power.

In desperation the Pan-African poured his pain into Black Power's thalamus. As he recovered he saw his opponent recoil. His right arm hung useless at his side and blood poured out of both nostrils. He channelled all of his power in the pain, all his resentment of this hero, this shining one. He punched Black Power in the centre of the chest. He felt the ribs go, the sternum crack.

The Pan-African reached out with his mind, found the small electric charge that gave rhythm to Black Power's heart and stopped it.

He held on for as long as he could, and that mighty heart struggled against him.

It got colder. The sun darkened and clouds gathered.

Wind.

Precipitation.

Snow.

The Pan-African collapsed.

## 2014

"I found him," said Lekan. "He spells his name "Phulani", like Fulani, but with ph. We're on. Black Power's in."

"He'll fight?" asked Tope.

"He was always going to fight," said Bank, not looking up from his tablet.

"To the death," said Lekan. "Signed the document, which you haven't, by the way."

"I'll get to that," said Tope. "How much did he want?"

"He said he'll fight you for free in a telephone booth in Tafawa Balewa Square, if need be."

"Hmm. Ali, *Boma ye.*"

Bank said, "Is a death match legal? Even in Nigeria?"

Lekan sucked his teeth. "My cousin is a councillor in Surulere. I'll get all the permits I need. We'll say the death match thing is only for publicity. If anything happens and one of you should... accidentally die, well, I'll bury the Lagos State governor in an ocean of Naira. Trust me, the bout will happen."

"And the dome?"

"It'll be a sphere. I've already commissioned my nephew to build it. Parts are already en route."

"How many of you are there?" asked Tope. "Your grandfather was pretty busy."

Lekan laughed. *"In a land where nepotism is currency, the man with plentiful relatives is god."*

"Don't be too sure," said Tope. "Do you know what Operation Deadwoods was?"

"No."

"1975. Nigeria's then Head of State Murtala Mohammed started Deadwoods to purge the corrupt officials from the government bureaucracy. He swept away hundreds of the unscrupulous civil servants and planned to return the country to civil rule."

"Hmm. And where did that get him?" asked Lekan.

## February 13, 1976
## Lagos, Nigeria

Presidential car, riddled with bullets, Murtala's cap on the back seat. The perpetuators, who hid sub-machine guns in their *agbada*, were gone.

Tope shook his head and flew away.

*You could have kept him alive, brother. I told you. I told you!*

This one time, Black Power responded:

*– Fuck off –*

## 2014

"An international airport and his face on a twenty-naira bill," said Bank.

Lekan snorted. "Murtala died for similar reasons to Lumumba. You played in that war theatre in the seventies, right? Murtala declared support for the MPLA. Any African leader who even smelled of Soviet or socialist leanings was a target for the CIA. Notice how Nigeria got a U.S style constitution soon after Murtala died?"

"I don't want to think about that time any more. When is the bout?"

"Six weeks to build the geodesic, five if I can get a hooker to blow my cousin." Lekan guffawed at his own wit.

"Which one?"

Elizabeth stirred and Tope felt the weight change on the bed. He opened one eye. She padded to his desk and opened the laptop. She punched a few keys and gasped.

He allowed himself the pleasure of ogling her fundament, then spoke: "What's wrong?"

She brought the screen to him. It was a tube video. A man forcefully kissed another man in a bar of some kind. Tope recognised the aggressor's face. The scene paused and a voiceover began commentary.

"The man in the video is Sipho Cele, a police detective. The smaller man in the picture is Colin Jordaan, and he has accused Detective Cele of rape. What is more astonishing is that Jordaan has alleged that Cele is the super powered adventurer from the seventies called Black Power."

The scene cut to an interview. Jordaan now sported several bruises, a black eye and a torn lower lip. "He walks around with this old, worn black mask in his pocket, fingering it for sexual pleasure. He was... I mean, I go to the gym, but there's no amount of resistance training that would make me strong enough to..." The man burst into tears.

The reporter said Detective Cele could not be reached for comment and it was unclear if he was under arrest.

"What do you make of it?" asked Elizabeth.

Tope didn't speak. He knew Black Power took male lovers from time to time, but rape? If he raped Jordaan the guy would be in hospital or a morgue, not on a TV show with minor bruises.

"This may not be what it looks like," said Tope.

"What? He's kissing a man."

"Yes, he is. That means he's gay or bisexual, but not necessarily a rapist."

"Will you fly over?"

Tope laughed. "When I went to prison one of the charges was violation of airspace. The other was flying in an urban area without a flight plan. Also, flying in a rural area without a flight plan. Flying without a permit. You get the etcetera? To do that, they first had to classify my body as an aircraft, then retrospectively charge me. It was a work of profound legal gymnastics. Bottom line is none of the Organisation of African Unity countries want me flying. So, no, I will not be flying to South Africa."

"Is it him?"

"The relevant question, Elizabeth, is how you knew about the video. I watched you. You woke and went straight to that web page without a search. What are you not telling me?"

Elizabeth stared at him.

"I can get it out of you if I want," said Tope. "But I want you to tell me."

She knelt back on her haunches, swallowed and said, "I have an implant."

"What kind?"

"It... I got it designed and needed thirty hours of surgery to have it inserted." She took his hand, parted her hair and ran his finger over the skin. He felt the bump. "That's the power supply. I have to change it every five years. It's experimental, but I had to have it. It cost fifteen million dollars and change."

"Again, what kind?"

"It keeps me connected to the Net wirelessly and sends the data to my sensory cortex. I can also feed data back down the same route. I see everything that goes on the net. I know everything. I bypass VPN tunnelling, software or hardware firewalls and one sixty-eight key bit triple DES encryption before breakfast."

"I don't know what that means."

"It means I can go anywhere on the internet, like God intended."

"You have a chip that helps you do that?"

"Yes."

"You're online all the time."

"Yes. Searching, cataloguing, looking for news as it happens. On people's mobile phones, on their fucking e-readers just because. I spent last night talking to eGhosts."

"What's an —"

"You know social media? Well, when people die in real life their online persona still exists, like their profiles, their email accounts, their blogs, their Tweets. This is an eGhost. If you amalgamate all the data, all the status updates, all the Tweets, you can pretty much construct a being who will respond and show quasi-independent thought."

Tope got up.

"Does this freak you out?" she asked.

"I don't know," said Tope. "You could have mentioned it."

"Why?"

"I don't know. I would have wanted... I don't know."

Elizabeth started getting dressed. "You know, you peer into people's heads and I trust you."

"I trust you."

"I don't see that from where I'm standing."

Soon, the door slammed.

She was gone.

# FOURTEEN

**2008**

**Alexandra Township, Johannesburg**

Killings.

More killings.

Just foreigners, they said, *kwerekwere*.

This was on a wide open field, stunted bushes bristling across from crumbling shacks and the firmer brick of township houses.

These had been people on their way to work perhaps, or just on their way somewhere, to talk, to have fun -- and not expecting to die.

Detective Cele bent down, looked at the two twisted, burnt bodies, with gathering rage. The site had been roped off, but a crowd stood watching, silent and sullen. The open field itself was partially scorched and baked blackish brown, smelling of dirt and charred meat.

He had to be detached and forensic about this, the support squad from his police unit combing the field for murder weapons; crusted blood from the corpses ragged head and torso wounds suggesting both *pangas* and *knobkieries*. Surprisingly, no guns.

Close quarter murders, personal and intimate. Cele gritted his teeth, he needed to be cool and professional, after all.

He stood up and shouted at the milling crowd: "You fucking bastards, why murder your own brothers and sisters?"

A slow growling noise from the mob, a faint echo of *umshini wami*, bring me my machine gun.

*You'll just tickle me with that,* Cele thought to himself. *And make me angry – and you won't like me when I'm angry.* A faint echo in that phrase, perhaps not his own?

A young police-woman came over, neatly uniformed, professional, holding out a partly burned bundle of papers. "ID documents, sir," she said.

He did not bother to take them. Wearily, "What nationality?"

"Not sure if they're from the victims, sir, but Mozambique and Malawian."

Not Nigerian. Not… his brother's people. Not yet, anyway.

He opened a sterile bag for her and she dropped the papers in, with black gloved fingers. He sealed lives away, with one thick brush of his thumb.

"Take this to the van," he said brusquely, "Call the meat squad in."

She almost curtsied deference – he was a senior detective who had been around for many years, after all. *Even more than you think, girl,* he thought, watching her bustle back to the van and wishing he could meet someone who would stand up to him, just a bit.

Like this crowd.

He walked towards the end of the plastic rope, pulled taut between two stakes, but with enough slack for him to stalk several metres into the crowd, without snapping. The mob moved back slowly, grumbling, ready to strike again.

He smiled, waiting for something to happen, fingering the mask in his pocket.

Slowly, in ragged groups, the crowd dispersed, trailing back to homes and places of meeting, a lucky few perhaps even to various jobs.

Behind him, bodies were removed.

But he could smell the muggy wind picking up now, lacings of moisture in the air as grey clouds boiled in from the horizon.

He stood, alone in the field, as rain lashed down on his face, cleaning the air and the ground. He could smell damp earth and sense the stirrings of worms beneath the ground, a few broken thorn trees in the distance standing out suddenly in the flares of sheet lightning.

*Life goes on*, he thought, *but is this only the beginning?*

All things start, but when will it end?

Shit, he's soaked – his suit will shrink on him if he's not too careful, time to go home.

Or, at least, just a place to sleep.

## 1975
## Cape Town

He could hear sounds on the Foreshore, near the docks, sounds that did not belong; the sound of deep drilling, within a bank filled with gold Krugerrands.

Intel had it that a foreign force had slipped in quietly to town, looking for easy pickings. There were no easy pickings on *his* watch...

There was a security van waiting for pick-up on the kerb outside, but he could tell the markings were fake, they had been sprayed a little too loosely, a little too unprofessionally. It took him one big bound to land on its roof, crushing and buckling it with the pounding weight of his feet and fists. There was a scream from a driver in the front carriage, a scream over breaking glass.

The white tellers and customers were calm when they saw him, splayed on the ground as they were, hands clasped above their heads. His mask and cape were well known around here, his power even more so – even though he had calmly stepped through the plate glass doors, showers of glass sliding off his impervious skin.

A semi-professional operation then, they at least had a man holding the forecourt of the bank, alert and armed, opening fire with fear, when he spotted the giant super-hero.

Black Power moved with easy speed – speed that no man could get a lock on. A left jab caved the man's skull, sending him sprawling across the polished floor in a spiral of blood, his gun mangled by a crunch from Power's right hand.

Deep inside the vaults, the drilling stopped.

Black Power bounded outside to land on the wrecked getaway van again, a man crawling away from the wreckage as sirens started to howl. Best keep the fight outdoors, where the chances for collateral damage was less.

A man stepped outside, and Black Power felt the weight of sudden unease. This man was tall, compactly built and walking with the ease of someone so capable as to fear very little.

"If you surrender now, I will spare you the might of Black Power," he boomed.

The man started and looked as if he were suppressing a laugh: "Brother, is that you?"

Black Power stepped off the broken van and approached cautiously. A tall man indeed, not much smaller than he, neatly dressed, but sporting a huge fuzz of head hair. His features were sharp, mobile, familiar...

It had been a long time.

A *very* long time.

"What the hell have you done to your hair?"

The man smiled: "It's called an Afro, you know, like the Jackson Five?"

Black Power snorted. "It looks ridiculous... Are you robbing this bank?" Three nervous, armed men stood behind his – brother.

"Brother, will you not greet me with a kiss? I haven't seen you in –"

"You were supposed to stay up north."

"I know. Things happened. I have been travelling around the world. I have much to tell you."

"You can tell me from jail. There can be only one penalty for breaking the law."

Cop cars were screeching to a halt nearby, but he waved them to a stop, he had this in hand.

"Brother, there is no need for violence. This money is going to feed women and children in Angola."

Black Power stamped forward, rippling a force wave through concrete, buckling the pavement, upending the three men, who fell with a clatter of weapons.

The tall man stood, several feet above the wrecked concrete pavement, hanging in the air like a mirage. Slowly, sadly, he shook his head – and then with a blur of speed, he was up into the sky, a speck disappearing amongst the few clouds leeching off the cloud cloth of Table Mountain.

*Brother, why have you turned back to crime?* thought Black Power pensively, as he strode into the bank hall again, where customers and tellers were picking themselves up.

They looked at him, but no one clapped.

"Ja sure, I know you don't allow black people in here – but your asses just got saved by a black man, so chew on that, honkeys."

He was met with blank looks. Of course, none of them would have seen *Shaft*, or anything like it. He sighed, feeling faintly ridiculous, knowing his brother would not be able to stop laughing, if he had watched and heard him just now.

*For both our sakes,* he thought grimly, *don't come back, brother.*

The police were moving past him now, careful not to touch him, heading for the vaults. One police man leveled a gun at the man lying against stairs at the far side of he hall, his broken automatic weapon crumpled like his body.

"Alamu," he'd heard a name mentioned. Yet again, black men die.

Black Power crouched low and then jumped, bursting through the roof in a spray of wood and brick, heading up and up, towards the Mountain, where no one would find or see him.

At least there, alone, hunched by yellow sandstone rocks and with an orange breasted sunbird calling nearby in the mountain fynbos, he began to feel somewhat at home again.

But his thoughts brooded north: 'Brother, after all these –
millennia – still the sharp tongue and the patronizing tone, even
though I am as yet ever the elder…'

## 2014
## Somewhere over Africa

Phulani Mabuza sat alongside Black Power in the specially commissioned SA jet, loaded with ANC government officials and a small, but selective, press entourage. Black Power, besides taking up two seats, wore a discreet grey track suit over his bodysuit, stitched in green letters on the back : 'Black Power' – he was *not* going to be mistaken for a British Petroleum flunkey again.

Phulani nodded to the Power's hand-luggage, a subdued but tall Italian leather man bag, well within luggage allowances.

"What you got in there, BP?"

Black Power leaned forward and flicked it open with his finger. He out a cowhide covered shaft and flat blade, about a metre in length, decorated with bright beads on the grip, balancing it on his fingers.

Phulani goggled at him, "What's that, a fucking *assegai?*"

"No," said Black Power, "An *iklwa* – Shaka himself gave it to me."

Phulani laughed then, clasping his suited belly, which had grown with the greying of his hair. "You always were a fucking clown, BP."

Black Power glowered at him through the mask.

Phulani unlaced his fingers and shifted back in his seat, a little nervously. He knew Black Power had limits to his tolerance, even though they went back as partners many, many years.

A young aspiring official from Foreign Affairs stood deferentially at their shoulders, a comic book in hand, holding it forward to be signed.

Black Power took it gently, knowing his fingers could shred the ageing yellow paper with the slightest of heavier touches.

"Ah –" he said, "The last issue." *Battle in the Sahara.* A few pen marks, crumpled spine, *VG at best*, he thought quietly to himself.

The official scurried off hurriedly – but with a pleased smile – holding the scrawled signature across the cover reverentially.

*No comic book violence coming up,* thought Black Power drily – and with a faint frisson of fear.

"What else you got in that bag there, BP?" asked Phulani, a little more relaxed, now that Black Power had signed his name on a collectible so cheerfully.

Black Power rummaged and pulled out a long cape, slowly and carefully.

"You – have – got – to – be – fucking – kidding – me," said Phulani.

The cape was a bright, luminescent rainbow in colour.

"Just making a statement," said Black Power.

"What," swallowed Phulani, "That you're representing the fucking rainbow nation?"

"And gay pride."

Slowly, Phulani shook his head, "Tell me it's a secret weapon to kill your brother by laughing until he chokes?"

Black Power shoved the cape back into the bag, almost bursting the bag's seams, which just about held, bulging, threatening to explode.

"You still miss Thendeka, don't you?"

Black Power was huddled forward, but still shot a sideways glance at Phulani, who had surprised him with the sensitivity in his comment. Not usual, nor in character, but Phulani had showed flashes of insights down the years, which had cemented the bumpiness of their years together. <u>And</u> he was a damn good fixer!

"Yes," he said shortly.

"Well, for fuck's sake, kiss another *woman* instead next time, okay?"

The plane's intercom system kicked in, as the aeroplane began to buck up and down with tropical turbulence and the seat belt signs pinged on.

"This is your captain speaking, we're about to head down towards the Murtala Muhammed International Airport."

"Fuck…" said Phulani, clasping the sides of his seat, "I wish we were going to watch the *Bafana Bafana* play the Super Eagles instead."

"Ha!" barked Black Power, "I stand a much better chance of winning this, than the *Bafana* would have."

Despite his words, Black Power suddenly felt very cold indeed, as the plane began its dip down towards Lagos.

# FIFTEEN

There was a crackle down the phone line that suggested either wind or that manoeuvre where the device is held between shoulder and ear, freeing the hand for other activities.

"I don't see him," said Bank.

"He's there," said Tope. "I can feel him. Hasn't been this strong in years."

"I'm telling you, I've seen all the flight data from Jo'burg. There is no listing."

"Look for a big Zulu-looking motherfucker with an entourage. He might be wearing sports clothes."

"Isn't he supposed to be under arrest?"

"Maybe, but I doubt it. The case was thin."

"I see him."

Tope took the image out of Bank's head. It took fifteen seconds to resolve the image. While doing that he picked up Bank's fear of being arrested as a terrorist for using field glasses in an airport. Boko Haram had been quiet, so it was reasonable to expect fireworks soon.

Bank was at the airport while Tope stayed home answering mail. Since the bout was announced all kinds of people sent all kinds of things for Tope to sign or touch and send back. They wanted him to contact their dead grandfather. They wanted to know who stole their money. They wanted to know if the baby was theirs, or if the baby was a boy, or if the baby had Sickle Cell Disease. Wasn't there a blood test for that these days? Hadn't these people heard of ultrasound?

It was Black Power all right. Age had made Cele slightly gaunt. His muscles didn't pop the way they used to, although nobody but Tope could notice such a difference. He wore a New York cap and an Addidas tracksuit. Duffel bag hooked around left shoulder. He did not look happy. Actually, he never looked happy.

"Actually, he never looked happy," said Bank.

Shit.

"Bank, I seem to be influencing your thoughts. It's not on purpose, but my control is a bit off. Try to think of a white screen."

"Just ignore the porn."

"I'm going to pretend I didn't hear that."

Weather forecast was good, temperature holding at a steady forty Celsius. Their presence together in the same geographic location hadn't caused any meteorological change. Yet.

"What's that in his hand?" asked Bank.

"It used to belong to Shaka Zulu. It's a weapon."

A priest once told Tope a story about Shaka Zulu. A white soldier told the great king that the manner in which the Zulu troops fought reminded him of the Spartans. He asked if Shaka had heard of them. Shaka asked if the Spartans died like other humans. The soldier asked what he meant. Shaka asked if, when pierced by a spear, the Spartans would cry out in pain. The soldier said he thought so. Then Shaka Zulu looked away from the soldier and said he had no use for such soldiers.

"If I command it my impi die in silence. These Spartans cry like women and give away their position," Shaka had said.

Tope smiled. Only Shaka kaSenzangakhona could call the Spartans pussies.

"Spartans pussies," said Bank.

Tope broke the link.

"Come home, Bank," said Tope.

Lekan hawked and spat.

"Yes, he's here. I didn't want to tell you yet because I didn't know if that rape allegation would go forward."

The dome was all but complete. It was a gigantic structure covered in scaffolding and bathed in Klieg lights. Construction continued day and night. Welding sparks floated slowly to the ground. Booms and cranes placed men in unusual positions over a hundred feet in the air.

"How's the foundation?" asked Tope.

"It's wedged in bedrock. Don't worry; it'll hold."

Lekan was happy, and he had good reason. He had already made one hundred million U.S. dollars in pay-per-view bookings alone. Advertising had not collated data yet and the gambling data was astronomical. Merchandising... the figures were beyond what Tope was used to or interested in.

Two men shuffled up in hardhats. They looked harried.

"Tope, I want you to meet Nick Wood and Tade Thompson."

"Pleasure," said Tope, but it sounded like a question. He wasn't sure what their role was. Both were slightly bookish, wore glasses and seemed in awe of him. Tade was black and Nick looked like he might be a Pacific Islander or mixed race, but both had that endomorphic look that Tope associated with academics.

"They're in charge of the novelisation," said Lekan.

"What novelisation?" said Tope.

"*Graphic* novelisation," said Nick. "We're immortalising the bout in print."

"Do you think you have the time to look at some character sketches?" said Tade.

Tope frowned at Lekan. "You know how I feel about this."

"*Pele, o!* Sorry. Look, I couldn't get at Orlando —"

"Orlando's dead," said Tope.

"That explains a lot," said Lekan.

Indeed. Orlando was rumoured to have been a consultant on the early MKDelta-sponsored Black Power comics, in addition to other African comics like South Africa's Mighty Man and Nigeria's Power Man. The projects all died off when CIA interference in Africa became unfashionable.

"We need some background information on you," said Nick.

"On both of you," said Tade. "The 1970s comics were simplistic bullshit."

They were both sweating and Tope got the impression they were not used to the warm climate. "Let's get some beers..."

The drums kept beating.

Tope was naked.

The *babalawo* sliced the cockerel's head off and sprinkled blood on Tope's head, all the while continuing with his monotonous incantations.

It was going to be a long night.

None of the rituals existed eight hundred years ago.

He saw Bank into the taxi.

"Uncle, are you sure you don't want me to –"

"I'm not coming back, Bank. One way or the other, this is it. Just share out the money the way I told you."

Bank's cheeks were wet with tears. "We will never forget you, Uncle."

"You better not! I made you all millionaires."

"I –"

"Just kidding. Go. Go now."

"You can win this."

"I can't kill him. He's my brother."

When the taxi pulled away, Tope felt the loss like a knife to the gut.

*Question: What do you do on the eve of your death?*

*Answer: Slot in a DVD and watch John McClane perforate European terrorists in a high rise building over one hundred and twenty frenetic, action-packed minutes!*

There weren't many people around the dome. It had no seating and was opaque so nobody could see anything but a dome during the fight. A security cordon went up weeks before and there was a desolate circle a mile wide around the arena. There were two doors, each coded to admit only one. The North face was for Black Power to enter, while the South was for Tope. There were no roads, and Tope flew up and dropped straight down on to the dome from orbit. The flames of re-entry died quickly against his force field.

He placed both palms against the south door and waited. It opened with a klaxon piercing the silence.

A shining walkway led to a metal platform in the centre.

Tope walked to the centre and sat cross-legged on the floor.

He closed his eyes and waited.

A sudden, loud vibration alerted him an hour later.

Black Power had landed.

*Morituri te salutamus.*

# SIXTEEN

**2014**
**Geodesic Dome, Lagos.**

Pan-African sat calmly, eyes closed, meditating.

But Black Power knew his presence has been marked...

...And that his brother was listening to him.

There would be no surprising him, they both knew each other too well.

Perhaps.

Power bowed, blanking his mind –

Jump, swing...

Pan-African rolled with his right hook, a glancing body blow, but still he gasped. Keep on him – left uppercut, right jab, scorpion kick, keep the fucker rolling and dodging, no time to think, no time to use his fucking mind.

Swivel kick, fucking sweet that one, sent him soaring into the top of this spherical dome, ramming him against the metal structure, blood spilling freely from his face. Jump now, nail the sucker...

*Shit, missed, uh! – these bars are titanium hard – losing that bastard to close quarters was a fucking mistake. Where's he –?*

Black Power grunted as he felt a rock hard fist ram into his midriff, and he started to fall, blows now raining against his face. *The sky's this fucker's space, air's his power, grab him, hold him, down to the ground...*

*Unhhhh, he's spun on top, using me like a fucking cushion – bastard's smaller, but still no fucking light weight. Off he goes again, ha – got his foot, swing him down – hard!*

The ground shook with the impact, blood flying again, as if in slow motion. Bounce him down hard again, his head fucking first this time.

Flashing red stars, stagger back, blink, one eye's puffed and gone, Pan-African's free again, must have kicked him hard in the face with his free leg. Tope, his brother, the younger, hangs on the edge of the cage, crouched, panting, bleeding.

Black Power could taste sour blood in his own mouth and strained to focus on the Pan-African with his good left eye, wiping blood from a cut leaking on his forehead.

*Fucking corny, those fight scenes in comics, when light repartee is exchanged. When it really gets down to it, each fucking word will cost you. Just get your breath back...*

It was then that he heard them.

A roar from the baying mob outside the cage, the audience packed in this huge open aired stadium, thousands upon thousands, baying them on, to kill each other. Millions more besides – probably several *billion* – watching, screaming, from across the digital globe.

*Whom should I be fighting,* Black Power thought, *and why am I fighting?*

"Lost your balls then?" Pan-African called, "Kissing too many men?"

*Fuck you,* he thought... *fuck everyone!!*

Black Power inhaled deeply, settling his weight squarely into his braced legs and haunches, summoning a focus of his strength, sweetly into his favoured left fist.

Pan-African steadied himself on the opposite wall, ready...

But he was not the target.

Black Power pivoted and drove his fist hard into the structure next to him – it stretched backwards, bent, buckled... exploded...

...and fragments of death flew everywhere...

Power opened his one good eye, feeling the ground beneath him shake and snap.

His brother, the Pan-African, hung in the air, blood pouring from a gaping wound in his chest. He appeared to be crying blood as he clenched his left fist – and Power could feel the ground lifting him up, fragments of the cage hanging like scattered, glowing ingots, caught in the might of the Pan-African's mental force field.

*Where the fuck's he going?* thought Black Power, as the air grew chill around them and the blue sky deepened into indigo, the ground now a very, very long way below them indeed...

# SEVENTEEN

**2014**
**Lagos, Nigeria**

Sixty-two miles above the surface.

*Dick Tiger once told me that boxing fights were abnormal. In fact, all sporting fights were abnormal. Fights in their natural state last seconds. Those that last longer than five minutes are usually between people who are not trying to hurt themselves.*

The fight took seconds. Forty-five seconds to cross the Karman line.

Forty-five seconds for Cele to cave the Pan-African's chest in.

*I am dying.*

*I am using micro-sized force fields to keep some of my blood in, but that won't save my life.*

*It's cold.*

*Black Power feels it too.*

*My mind can keep the platform up here long enough to freeze his blood.*
*We both die.*

*Check, mate and fuck you, brother.*

*Elizabeth...*

*Elizabeth...*

The remnants of the geodesic dome fell to the earth as a meteor shower, red hot chunks of titanium which set off forest fires and destroyed houses.

Seventy-one people lost their lives.

The Pan-African's body burnt up in re-entry, lacking a force field to protect it.

\*

114

Black-Power was frozen, then burned, then broken against the Earth's surface. His suit was carbonised and the skin blackened and peeled off.

Trees still blazed around him. He tried to stand but his muscles would not obey. He remembered being struck by lightning three times during his descent, each hit like the accusing finger of God.

He could not cry – his tear ducts were gone. He could barely see. His harm-resistant eyelids had been able to protect his corneas only so much. The left was scorched, but the right had better light perception.

He sensed someone close by.

"Are you proud of yourself, old man?" said Thembeka. "A little fratricide to prove you still have lead in your pencil?"

"Thembeka…"

"He was kin to us. I could feel it…"

Black Power could not see her clearly but he felt the rage coming off her. He tried to speak, coughed instead. The fire had gone down his throat. He could rasp, though.

"Thembeka, fuck off. We are not related to you, Tope and I."

She edged close to his ear.

"*Were*, asshole. You mean 'we were not related' not 'are'. Tope is dead, remember?"

The pain threading his nerves intensified and he gasped, clutching at air.

"Shit, Power, you're a fucking absolute mess," she cradled his head then; held him.

"Thendeka," he croaked, "I'm sorry." All he could smell was burning, and the all-consuming pain threaded itself tighter and tighter into his body, constricting his throat.

"Shhhhh," she said, "I can *hear* you. So… you *did* love him, once."

"Yes," he said.

Black Power wished he could cry. Instead, he managed a painful croak. Thendeka poured some water onto his lips and tongue. He coughed his thanks.

"You forgive me?" he managed.

"No," she said. "It's not that easy."

A strange weather formation over Africa.

Several listening posts were already turned towards the continent as a precaution in case the bout between suprahumans developed complications, so it was well documented. The clouds seemed to be on fire, but it later became clear. A wormhole terminated there and left a ship, some said a shuttle.

It looked like a grand, black metal spider. It flew as if light, but the earth reverberated when it touched down above the spot where Black Power lay against Thembeka.

The woman tensed for battle.

"At ease," said Black Power. "I know this ship. I remember now. It's me they want."

Two constructs emerged, shining ones like Biblical burnished brass men. Black Power struggled to his feet and accepted the inhibitor bracelets, starting to go with his gaolers.

"What are you?" asked Thembeka.

"A criminal," croaked Black Power. "Protect them, Thembeka. I always wanted to…"

"When you weren't trying to forcibly copulate with them," she said, but the fire was gone from her eyes, "What was your crime?"

He looked down. "Forcing myself sexually on others."

She laughed then. And cried.

He held out his blackened mask. "Please, carry on. You will do better than me."

"I don't need that," she said, "I won't hide behind that. I am now a member of 'Behind the Mask'; we fight for the rights of people of all sexualities within Africa… But, is there any chance I could get your rainbow cape, the one you never fought with?"

"Phulani told you, the bastard," Black Power cracked a painful smile, "Sure — *sala kathle*, sister."

"Goodbye to you too, detective."

Black Power's last words floated over his shoulder, as he entered the ship: "*Umuntu Ngumuntu Ngabantu.*"

Thembeka smiled — a human becomes human, through being with others.

The ship rose, the burning cloud phenomenon happened again, and then it was over.

"...And then it was over," said Thembeka. "That was the end of Black Power, returned to interstellar incarceration somewhere left of the I-don't-give-a-fuck solar system."

Elizabeth Kokoro stopped typing and saved the document. She switched off the recorder.

"You were in love with him," said Thembeka. "I can feel it."

"I think I loved them both," said Elizabeth. "And hated them too."

They both laughed until they cried.

"What are you going to do?" asked Thembeka.

"A book. *The Last Pantheon.* You just helped me finish it and I already have a publication deal secured. What of you?"

Thembeka went to the window and opened it.

"Fight crime," she said. "What else is there for people like me?"

The curtain fluttered.

She was gone.

# ABOUT THE AUTHORS

**Tade Thompson** is a writer of novels, short stories and screenplays in ddition to being a full time consultant psychiatrist. He is best known for *Rosewater* and *The Murders of Molly Southbourne*, both of which have been optioned for adaptation. He has won the Arthur C. Clarke Award, the Nommo Award, the Kitschies Golden Tentacle Award, the Utopiales award, and the Julia Verlange Award among others. He has been a Hugo Award and Shirley Jackson Award finalist.

Born in London to Yoruba parents, he lives on the south coast of England.


**Nick Wood** (1961 – 2023) was a South African-British clinical psychologist and Science Fiction writer, with over twenty published short stories to his credit. His highly acclaimed debut novel, *Azanian Bridges* (NewCon Press, 2016), was shortlisted for four Awards: the Sidewise, Nommos , the BSFA and the John W. Campbell awards. Nick's follow up, *Water Must Fall* (NewCon Press, 2020) is a near future, solar-punk thriller, positing the question: in a world of disappearing water, who gets to drink? Nick's short story collection, *Learning Monkey and Crocodile* (Luna Press, 2019), gathers together a powerful set of Ecological SF stories.

Nick passed away unexpectedly in June 2023, having suffered with increasingly debilitating chronic medical conditions in his latter years.

# GENESIS OF THE PANTHEON

## The Initial Email Exchange

**5.22 pm, February 10th 2013**
**Tade Thompson**

Hi, Nick,

Since we had that discussion on Afro-Punk Collective this weekend about African superheroes an idea has been swimming round in my head. Okay, so hear me out fully before you make up your mind. Now, the concept of the superhero in Western nations/civilisations has been deconstructed ad nauseum. *Watchmen, Dark Knight Returns, Killing Joke*, etc. We get it.

I think that the African superhero deserves a similar deconstruction and farewell.

Here's what I'm thinking: how would you feel about collaborating on a project? It would be an illustrated novella that closes the chapter on the African superhero.

A kind of where they are now, how did they get there, what was the socio-political context and consequence of their existence etc. We could look into the aspect of them being a weak copy of American heroes, maintaining the status quo, whether this favours Africans or not.

This would be an illustration-heavy book (think *Resurrection Man* by Sean Stewart)

We'd share the writing chores. Everything would be 50-50 including any profit, critical acclaim, or notoriety that might result.

Please understand, I see this as a chance for both of us to tell a story that (I think) we both care about.

Okay (breathless). So. What do you think?


**9.12 am, February 11ᵗʰ 2013**
**Nick Wood**
Sounds an interesting idea, Tade – do you know if there were any other African heroes touted apart from 'Power Man' and 'Mighty Man' – of course, Marvel had their Americanised version in the Black Panther, but I'm thinking of heroes actually situated and published within Africa...?

# INTERVIEW WITH TADE THOMPSON IN BOOKSIY

**First, I wanted to congratulate you both on your novels -** *Making Wolf* **and** *Azanian Bridges* **– but would you be willing to talk about how the idea for** *The Last Pantheon* **came about?**

**Tade**: Nick and I belonged to the now-defunct Facebook group The Afro-Punk Collective. In February 2013 there was a rather detailed discussion about superheroes in general and African superheroes in particular. Prior to this, Nick had written a well-received article about African comics.

I approached Nick with the idea of a collaboration. The initial motive was deconstruction of the African superhero, a topic it was obvious we both cared about. It was also a love-letter to a medium that the literary establishment often dismisses as kids' stuff. At this time we did not really know each other except by our work in the first AfroSF anthology.

**What was it like working together on** *The Last Pantheon?*

**Tade**: You hear horror stories about collaborations. You hear about ego clashes and deadline problems and decisions to discontinue.

This, however, was painless. It was like we both had the same background in comics, the same narrative priorities, the same socio-cultural rage at the depiction of Africa in mass-media.
I do not recall a single disagreement. If anything, the collaboration led to us meeting each other's families and becoming friends.

**(This is a 2-part question) I found** *The Last Pantheon's* **approach to Africa's political history through superheroes very interesting.**

a) **Why that focus for the story?**

**Tade**: Because *The Last Pantheon* is not really a superhero story. It's really a commentary on how African history is neglected. In mainstream stories what you find is the Western version of the "History of the World" is revised and rehashed again and again. I always wonder why any flashbacks to "world" history always highlights Hitler as the ultimate evil, but says nothing about Leopold II.

Obviously we could not revise all of the history of the continent, but we wanted some touchstones relevant to our respective cultures.

We wanted the African reader to feel important, and we wanted the Western reader to become curious if the names and events were unfamiliar.

b) **Do you think BlackPower and Pan-African could have also played a more crucial role in our history if i) they weren't so caught up in their own feud; and ii) one wasn't so neutral?**

**Tade**: Possibly. But the nature of the superhero narrative is flawed and perhaps rooted in adolescent power fantasies. You can't solve your problems by punching them (or someone). One of the themes of the novella is the futility of using violence to solve your problems. Each time our heroes tried to intervene they either did not intervene early enough, or they failed outright. The Cold War in the late 60s and 70s played out in black Africa with wars, extra-judicial assassinations and coups that were thinly-veiled CIA plots. There was no easily-identifiable supervillain to incapacitate with energy bolts.

(This is also a 2-part question) *The Last Pantheon* also clearly pays homage to comic book series, some of which you mention in the story – Mighty Man and PowerMan.

a) **Was there something particular about those two comics? And did they influence the creation of Black Power and Pan-African?**

**Tade**: The comics had a similar genesis, and a similar hold on our respective imaginations. I read Powerman (also known as Powerbolt) as a child in Lagos. What I later found out is that while the funds were Nigerian, the creative team was British (Comics legend Dave Gibbons actually asked the moneymen why they did not use local talent, but received no satisfactory answer). That aside, I read American comics mostly. We would buy them from Kingsway Stores, but they did not appear with any regularity. Powerman did. It was not the only comic. There was 'Super 8' and 'Benbella' (which was created locally).

I should point out that both Powerman and Mightyman were anthology comics, and they both had several backup comics in common. For example, Jake 'Wonderboy' Masala was a boxing strip. There was also a cowboy strip called 'Django' I think.

These comics told stories that were relevant to our day-to-day lives. They spiritually influenced Black Power and Pan-African.

**b)** **Also, were there any other influences (comic books or otherwise)?**

**Tade**: Heh, how much time do you have? *Pantheon* is the condensed effect of possibly hundreds of influences. I mean, one has to start with the late Jack Kirby; The works of Alan Moore and Grant Morrison; Morak Oguntade and Tayo Fatunla are two Nigerian cartoonists whose work I consumed every day in my teenage years; the writer D.O Fagunwa for the novel *Forest of a Thousand Daemons*; the writer Kola Onadipe; Flora Nwapa; Dambuzo Marechera etc.

**Final question: what's next?**

**Tade**: My science fiction novel *Rosewater* set in a futuristic Nigeria comes out in September 2016 from Apex Books. I also have a novella and two short stories scheduled for publication this year. I'm writing a follow-up to *Making Wolf* as well as an urban fantasy novel set in London. Busy year!

# BUILDING SUPER-HEROES

## Nick Wood
BSFA Focus Magazine, Summer 2019

Tade and I co-wrote an African super-hero saga "The Last Pantheon" for *AfroSF vol. 2*. We'd had a prior discussion on the history of super-heroes in Africa and, excitedly, found we were on the same page, albeit coming from different backgrounds. For more information on African superheroes, see Tessa Pijnaker (2018)'s discussion: African Superheroes in the 70s and 80s: https://africainwords.com/2018/06/11/african-superheroes-in-the-1970s-and-80s-a-historical-perspective/

I was initially anxious about our agreement to co-write our own version of an African superhero tale – mostly because one of the attractions of solo writing for me, is being in control of own world, i.e. I'm able to build – or break down – any wall I wanted to. How can it work, when relinquishing such dictatorial control? But I decided it might be an important writing lesson for me to give up some control and learn to respond to someone else's cue and lead. I had been finding it increasingly hard to write on my own, as the blank screen was growing ever more aversive in my mind, so I thought, what is there to lose? I waited for Tade to kick off – and when he did, I thought, wow! Now that's interesting, how can I respond to his Nigerian superhero/villain, Pan-Africa? Snow in the Sahara? Now that, I did not expect. There was something in his (to me) left field start, that triggered a wider shower of ideas for responding, than had I been writing alone. How can my South African super-hero (Black Power) respond, given the setting and the launching action – for this is obviously a bigger Pan-African saga than I had initially anticipated? It was as if Tade had burst the blank screen open into a Wide-Screen movie. (It probably helped that, like Alex Latimer above, Tade is also a visual artist.)

Over the course of several weeks per chapter we swapped the progressing interaction between his pan-African and my Black Power. We respected each other's chapters and did not edit each other, nor did we provide too much guidance as to where we wanted the story to go.

This was right out of my comfort zone and I was anxious it might fizzle into a plot dead-end, but while the character's and their supporting cast still fizzled together on the screen, it felt reassuring to continue. The chapters bounced back and forth between us, like a literary ping_pong ball and I grew increasingly excited and less anxious about where we might go next.

It took one final face-to-face meeting, after our initial Skype meeting where we had agreed the project, to iron out the conclusion. We did have a slight difference of opinion as to the ending and we drafted a few versions before finally agreeing, together, what felt like the best one. It felt important that we 'honour the story' by pushing through our differences until we could finally generate an ending that we were both happy with. By the agreed end of *The Last Pantheon*, I realised I had never once feared the blank screen. There was something in the creative synergy that meant ideas and words were kept circling between us, and alive. I think part of that came from a shared passion of the topic, an enjoyment of each other's writing - but also crucially, at the end, a willingness to disagree, challenge and search together for a better ending, for the shared characters we had both grown to love.

As can be seen from these three experiences there is no one right way to co-write – from Alex writing (and mapping) the plots and Diane adding the bulk of the words, to Tade and I swapping equally weighted chapters that progressed a character driven (implicit) narrative arc. Trust, respect and a willingness to listen are all parts of a successful collaboration. Of course, it could have gone pear-shaped as well, there is no guarantee of success attached to any co-operative venture. For example, if we had deadlocked on the ending, each wanting our own initial version, the story may not have survived. Joint writing does indeed involve giving up some degree of control – but, as I learned during this venture, that's not necessarily a bad thing!

But, in the end, if a co-operative venture works well – hopefully like this three-authored article – you end up with a narrative that feels stronger than the sum of its parts. So next time you are sitting with an empty screen in front of you, don't let it get into your head, why not open yourself to collaborating instead? You may even learn new ways of approaching the writing of SFF.

# THE LAST WORD ON THE LAST PANTHEON

## Tade Thompson

Whenever a new African superhero or comic is announced, I prepare myself to be irritated. The inevitable reviews or interviews will no doubt say something like this is the first superhero from the Dark Continent or Africa is finally opening up to the science fiction world or some such. It irritates me that they do not research the topic before writing the piece. There have been African superheroes since the early 70s.

On February 18, 1979 in Algiers, it snowed in the Sahara for about an hour. This factoid remained in my head for decades, but I always thought it would be a good starting point for a story. Two gods battling it out and hitting each other so hard that for a time the weather becomes deranged.

This guy called Nick Wood wrote an article on an African superhero called Mighty Man and he was speaking my language. Nick and I had been in the AfroSF Anthology, and we both belonged to The Afro-Punk Collective Facebook group, so in 2013 I reached out to him. We had a long discussion about superheroes and African history and comics. The germ of the idea for The Last Pantheon came when Nick toyed with the idea of writing an article about the lost African superheroes. That evolved into us deciding to write a story together. We didn't talk of length, but it was to be about deconstructing the African hero and fully illustrated. Ahh, ambition. How cute. That didn't happen.

Somehow, things we felt strongly about kept coming up. The secret wars of the CIA in Cold War Africa, the killing of Patrice Lumumba, the Rumble in the Jungle between Muhammad Ali and George Foreman, Kwame Nkrumah, the Pan-African movement, the violence in Angola, the murderous legacy of Leopold II, von Daniken's *Chariots of the Gods?* hoax, MK Ultra, MK Delta, and a whole lot of American comic book lore with which we were both familiar. What is a superhero, really? Why beat up criminals? *Cui bono?* Is the beloved caped, steroidal tights-wearing powerhouse not just another way of maintaining a status quo that requires examination? We also thought since the Cold War was playing out, we could incorporate the concept of MAD: Mutually Assured Destruction. This was the Pig Iron from which The Last Pantheon emerged.

The comic characters we were trying to pay homage to were Mighty Man, who was a South African pastiche of early, 'single-bound' Superman, and Powerman, who was an African analogue of Silver Age Superman, except his weakness was snakebite (but cured by electricity). We thought since African superheroes are largely unknown to the West, it would be better to have archetypal characters for easy recognition. We even had shorthand like 'Loisalike character' which is self-explanatory. I did some concept art in India Ink, and you can find some of it around the Net. It's possible we will release it later as a standalone Deluxe edition which will be illustrated as God intended.

Since Nick knows South Africa and I know Nigeria, we decided to set the story in both. We also decided to each take one of the main protagonists and write their backstory and dialogue, to give an individual feel. We wrote the chapters in a round-robin fashion, giving each other only broad strokes of a plot. It was an amazing collaboration. We used email, telephones and Skype. We did not have a single disagreement and became friends in the process, meeting each other's families. Let's just say literary or artistic collaborations have a history of not being pleasant, and we were both worried at the start, but it turned out well. When we finished the first draft we had a meeting in a North London café to discuss revision of the entire book.

We had to cut a few things because we didn't know how it would affect people. For example, comic legend Joe Orlando was involved in the African comics of the 70s and there was a whole conspiracy sub-plot which I was invested in, but Nick wisely declared to be risky. There was a long bit about them inspiring some of the legends and gods of different African pantheons, but we truncated it. We did make them a bit like gods in that they would need worshippers in order to manifest their powers, which led to the TV interview being a source of power, since viewers would now think of them.

Nick wanted to submit to Tor.com, which was sensible, but I said we almost had a duty to submit to *AfroSFv2*. We also considered self-publishing; which was not out of the question. We deliberately left the ending so that the story could be continued, preferably by a female writer or writers. Onwards, to the Super-Women of Africa too!

My novel *Rosewater* is a near-future science fiction story set in Nigeria, and is released form Apex Books in September 2016. I also have a novella called *Gnaw* from Solaris Books later this year. I'm also working on the sequel to my alternate history noir novel *Making Wolf* (which just won a Golden Tentacle for best debut novel at the Kitschies). Nick has an alternative history novel *Azanian Bridges* coming out this Easter, set in a current South Africa where apartheid has survived. Together, we both care about helping to hoist the banner of African SFF.

The last word?

AMANDLA!

# ALSO FROM NEWCON PRESS

### Best of British Science Fiction 2022 – Donna Scott

Editor Donna Scott has scoured magazines, anthologies, webzines and obscure genre corners to discover the very best science fiction stories by British and British-based authors published during 2022. A thrilling blend of cutting-edge and traditional, showcasing all that makes science fiction the most entertaining genre around

### Saving Shadows – Eugen Bacon

Speculative micro-lit by award-winning author Eugen Bacon. Forty-eight pieces, twenty-two of which are original to this book. Complementing the stories are a series of full page illustrations commissioned by the author from artist Elena Betti; thirty-five stunning images that enhance the reading experience.

### Polestars 3: The Glasshouse – Emma Coleman

Contemporary tales of rural horror and dark fantasies steeped in folklore from one of genre fiction's best kept secrets. A young divorcee relocates to a quaint rural hamlet but is mystified by the hostility of her neighbours…A man discovers an item in a junkshop that puts him in fear of his life… An impresario dispenses justice while performing as a magician…

### Polestars 4: Our Savage Heart – Justina Robson

The first collection in twelve years from one of the UK's most respected and inventive writers of science fiction and fantasy. 100,000 words of high quality fiction, that gathers together the author's finest stories from the past decade, including a brand new piece written especially for this collection.

### Polestars 5: Elephants in Bloom – Cécile Cristofari

Debut collection from a French author who has been making a name for herself with regular contributions to *Interzone* and elsewhere. Providing a fresh perspective on things, Cécile's fiction reflects her love of the natural world and concern for its future. Contains her finest previously published stories and a number of brand new tales that appear for the first time.

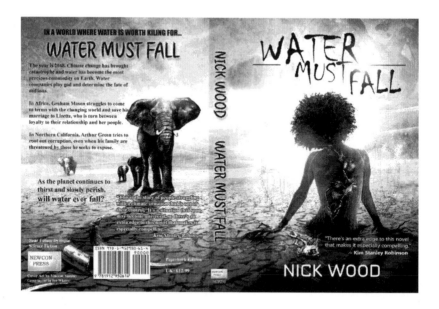

The year is 2048. Climate change has brought catastrophe and water has become the most precious commodity on Earth. Water companies play god and determine the fate of millions.

"This is the story of people struggling with a climate situation that is out of their control and yet determines everything about their lives. It's a situation that soon may become universal, so there's an extra edge to this novel that makes it especially compelling."
                                    – *Kim Stanley Robinson*

"…it extrapolates the inequalities and politics of today into a future where climate-catastrophe has created a world where even water is scarce. Yet the book is one of hope – of building new communities and systems, of learning, of family, of new forms of consciousness and of how we, and the world, can change."
                                    – *Wole Talabi in The Guardian*

"Nick Wood's futuristic cli-fi is a layered political drama that races you across a maze of suspense-filled intrigue." – *Aurealis*

www.newconpress.co.uk